Lay That Trumpet in Our Hands

A Stage Play
By Kris Vosler

Adapted From the Novel
"Lay That Trumpet in Our Hands"

By Susan Carol McCarthy

Contact Info:
Kris Vosler
krisvb@umich.edu
www.krisbauske.com

Cast of Characters

Reesa McMahon	14 year old white girl and daughter of the only Yankee family in a southern citrus town in Central Florida. Marvin is her best friend before his murder. Reesa is a nickname for Marie Louise.
Marvin Cully	19 year old black man. Marvin and his father work for Marie Louise's family, and they are like family to each other. Marvin is killed early in the play, and the character becomes Marie Louise's memories of Marvin, popping up at odd times to discuss the action.
Warren McMahon	White father of Reesa in his early thirties. He cannot use his right arm much ~ a result of polio contracted the year Reesa was born. Still, he is strong and determined.
Elizabeth McMahon	Early thirties white mother of Reesa. She is pretty and has a quiet strength. Homemaker, she helps out with the family citrus business. She is the doubter. She loved Marvin, but she's not sure if it's worth the risks to find his killer.

Dot	Marie Louise's grandmother who lives near Chicago but visits every winter. Dot is in her early fifties but spry and active. She is attractive and outspoken and wears cat's eye glasses. She arrives in Central Florida shortly after Marvin is killed and plays a large part in bringing down the Klan.
Luther Cully	Black male, 42. Father of Marvin. Luther is also a music minister at this church and heads a spy ring made up of choir members to help bring down the Klan.
Armetta Cully	Black female, 37. Mother of Marvin. Friend of the McMahon family.
Thurgood Marshall	Lawyer for the NAACP out of New York City during the fifties. He is a large black male with both an easy smile and a very serious demeanor. He is likened to a big bear and, like a bear, he is both cuddly and dangerous. 43 years old in 1951. He wears a suit and tie.

Harry T. Moore	Black male who headed the NAACP in Florida. He is smaller than Marshall but equally as committed to their cause. He is 46 in 1951. He wears a suit and tie as well.
Lucy Garnet	Wife of a Klansman in denial.
Mary Sue	White waitress at a local restaurant. Southern accent. (May double Lucy Garnet/Iris.)
Lakeview Inn Hostess	Pleasant white woman in her middle years. She has worked at the Inn a long time and remembers Mrs. McMahon. (May double as Mz. Lillian.)
Deputy Donnelly	Large, overweight, white southern male. Member of KKK. (May double Emmett Casselton.)
John Ivey	White male member of the Klan. Very tall and thin. Carries himself hunched over ~ strong southern accent.

Morris Bellview	White, member of the Klan.. He has dark hair and a bald spot ~ strong southern accent.
Mz. Lillian/Hostess	She is a white middle-aged southern woman of the fifties. She owns the local beauty shop. (May double hostess at the Lakeview Inn.)
Iris	Early twenties, white woman who works at the beauty shop. Strong southern accent. (Double with Lucy Garnet and Mary Sue.)
Mr. Jameson	White, northern agent for the FBI trying to bring down the Klan.
Emmett Casselton	Large, imposing white man with a thick southern accent. He is arrogant and used to being in control. Older male, 50 – 60.
Radio Announcer	White male voice on the radio. (May double John Ivey or Morris Bellview.)

ACT I

Scene 1

AT
RISE:

Evening inside the McMahon
Family home. It is a simple single
story house in Central Florida in the
spring of 1951. The pretty kitchen
is stage left with a back door at the
rear of the stage. A window looks
out on a citrus tree in full bloom in
the yard also stage left.
A comfortable living room with no
television is center stage. An old
piano has a place of honor in the
room. REESA'S bedroom is stage
right. It is not fancy or frilly, but it
is comfortable.
REESA McMAHON (14) is in her
bedroom. Her father WARREN
McMAHON is adjusting the
window as Reesa snuggles under
her covers. She is nearly tucked
into bed, when she sits up to discuss
something with her father. She is
wearing a modest white cotton
nightgown. He wears the clothes of
a grove worker in 1951.

REESA
Daddy, why does Billy Merkle keep
calling me a Yankee?

WARREN
Why do you think he calls you a Yankee?

REESA
Because we don't sound the same when
we talk?

WARREN
That's part of it. Your mother and I were
both born in Illinois, so we missed out on
that soft southern drawl.

REESA
But President Truman was born in
Missouri, and Billy doesn't call him a
Yankee.

WARREN
(chuckles)
Only because he hasn't had the chance,
Reesa.

REESA

And I was born right here in Plymouth ~
just like Billy!

WARREN

Ahhh… You may have been born here,
but you have our Yankee values. You
think like us. You certainly speak like us.
I guess that makes you a Yankee too.
Sorry, Reesa.

REESA

I don't mind. I'd rather be like you than
Billy Merkle any day. It's just… he says
it like it's a bad thing.

WARREN

Most folks who live in these parts have
had family here since before the Civil
War, Reesa. They don't know any better.

REESA

Better than what?

WARREN

They just think differently about things
than we do.

REESA

Like the Klan?

WARREN

I've told you before, the Klan's nothing more than a bunch of ridiculous men dressing in sheets to scare people. Like the Boogey man!

REESA

Billy says anybody who's anybody's a member of the Klan, and only Yankees like us would have colored foreman running our grove.

WARREN

That may be true in Billy Merkle's world, but we didn't have the Klan where I grew up near Chicago, Reesa. The Klan stands for a lot of things I can't abide. Always better to be a Yankee than a Klanner. It's been nearly ninety years since the Civil War ended, and some of those boys are still fighting over the color of a man's skin.

REESA

What's that got to do with anything?
Luther's the best foreman around, and
Marvin's my best friend. I never thought
twice about the color of their skin.

WARREN

You don't know how happy I am to hear
that, Reesa.

REESA

Billy doesn't call them 'colored' like we
do, Daddy. He uses the word you…

WARREN

The word I hate. There are reasons we
don't use that word, Reesa. A man is a
man, and any man worth his salt deserves
to be called a man and nothing else!

REESA

Next time Billy Merkle makes a crack
about me being a Yankee, I'm going to
tell him I'm proud to be a Yankee. Better
to be Yankee than a Klanner!

WARREN

You do that, Reesa! You do that!

REESA
(hugs Warren)
Good night, Daddy. Love you!

WARREN
(steps to door)
Love you too, Reesa. Reesa?

REESA
Mmmmm?

WARREN
I'm glad you're a Yankee.

REESA
(sleepily)
Me too, Daddy. Me too. Tell Mamma I
said good night.

*He turns out the light and heads down the hall to his own
room. The house is dark and quiet until there is a
pounding on the door. Director may choose to light the
clock hanging on the wall in the kitchen to show the
passage of time, or use a spotlight to represent a full
moon which passes slowly over the house, visible
through the windows, before Luther appears. Six hours
pass between Reesa's bedtime and Luther's arrival. A*

dim spot stays on Reesa who sits bolt upright when a tapping is heard on the back door. LUTHER peers in through the curtains at the window in the door. He waits a moment and taps again. A light goes on down the hall from Reesa's bedroom, and Warren appears. He pulls up his suspenders and drags on a shirt as he walks to the kitchen. Luther taps again. ELIZABETH, wearing a dressing robe, follows Warren. Reesa watches them through a small crack she opens at her bedroom door. When the lights go on in the kitchen, she follows to see what's going on.

WARREN
I'm a coming. Hold on.

(Warren flips on the light, and opens the door. Luther enters)

LUTHER
Sorry to bother you so late, MistaWarren.

WARREN
Luther, please, I've told you not to call me Mister. We've been friends too long.

LUTHER
Sorry, MistaWarren. You know I can't do that. People hears that, they start

thinkin' ol' Luther's getting' to be an uppity nigger, and then *I'd* have trouble with the Klan.

                    WARREN
                    (sighs with resignation)
Too late in the season for a freeze, Luther. What is it?

                    LUTHER
Cain't say for sure anything's wrong, MistaWarren. Just a feeling I got. That's all.
(Nods at Elizabeth as she enters the kitchen and gets out coffee and the coffee pot, and starts making hot coffee.)
Evenin', Miz'Lizbeth.

                    ELIZABETH
Evening, Luther. Looks like morning's just around the corner.

                    LUTHER
That it is.

                    WARREN
What kind of feeling?

(Reesa stumbles into the kitchen sleepily and sits
down in one of the chairs at the kitchen table.
She listens with curiosity.)

                    LUTHER
        Well, Marvin ain't come home yet,
        MistaWarren, and you know that boy.
        Ain't like him to be late. Armetta's 'bout
        worried herself to death. The boy went
        out 'round eight, telling his mamma he'd
        be back 'fore midnight. Ah been lookin'
        for him since one.

                    WARREN
        What time is it now?

                    LUTHER
        After four. Run into Jimmy Lee just now.
        Swears he saw Klanners cruisin' the Trail
        where Marvin's s'posed to be.

                    WARREN
        The Klan? Where on the Trail?

                    LUTHER
        There's a girl up by Zellwood. He's been
        spending time at her place some evenin's,
        but he's always back by twelve.

WARREN
Marvin had any run-ins with the Klan?

LUTHER
No sir, but the girl say he left 'round
'leven.

WARREN
What do you think?

LUTHER
(talking grown up code in front of Reesa)
I'm hopin' we could check on Mistuh
Myer's Valencia grove ~ drive slow-like
past Round Lake. Take a look.

WARREN
Come on in. I need to get my shoes on
and some coffee.

ELIZABETH
(worried)
Coffee's on, Warren. It'll just be a
minute.
(She touches his elbow. They are both deeply
concerned.)
Want a cup for the road, Luther?

LUTHER

No thank you, Miz'Lizbeth.

WARREN

Elizabeth, you might as well go back to bed. You too Reesa. Nothing for you to worry about.

REESA

Can I come, Daddy? I'll be dressed quick as a wink.

WARREN

No, you can't come. We don't know what's out there. Crawl back under the covers for a while. Besides, Grandma's coming today. Aren't you supposed to be watching for the DeSoto?

LUTHER

Your mamma comin' in today?

WARREN

Yep, we get her for Easter this year.

LUTHER

She somethin', Miz Dot is. And that car!

WARREN

Suits her perfectly, doesn't it?

ELIZABETH

(hands Warren a thermos)
Here's the coffee. I put the sugar in the
thermos. Just give it a shake.

WARREN

(grabs a hat and coat from the peg by the door)
Come on, Luther. Better get going.
We'll take the truck.

LUTHER

Thank you, MistaWarren. Sorry to bother
you MizLizbeth. Reesa.

WARREN

Don't worry, Lizbeth. Bye, Roo! Don't
forget the hospital corners on Dot's bed.
(They exit. Roar of the old truck motor is heard
disappearing into the distance.)

REESA

Where on Round Lake?

ELIZABETH

Reesa

(sighs)

There's been talk about a lemon grove ~
one of Mr. Casselton's, but…

REESA

Emmett Casselton? King of Casbah
Groves?

(eyes widen with awareness and fear)

Mamma, you mean they've taken Marvin
to the Casbah!?

ELIZABETH

I don't know, Reesa. I doubt it. Anyhow,
what do you know about going to the
Casbah?

REESA

Billy Merkle says when the Klan takes
someone to the Casbah, they never go
home again. Is Marvin going to be okay,
Mamma?

ELIZABETH

(puts on a strong face)

I don't know. I do know however, neither
one of us in getting back to sleep now. In

the time it'll take me to fix your
breakfast, you can finish your
grandmother's bed. Go on now. I'll call
you when it's ready.

*Elizabeth gets out a pot and a box of oatmeal.
Reesa exits to the hallway between the living
room and bedrooms. She opens a closet door
and takes out fresh, pink sheets. She disappears
into the bedroom behind hers which is not visible
to the audience. Reesa uses this opportunity to
change into her day clothes. Lights dim on Reesa
as she exits. Elizabeth sets the bowl of oatmeal
on the table with a spoon and a napkin. She
walks down the hall to her bedroom. Elizabeth
removes her robe which conceals her day clothes
to make time seem to have passed when she and
Reesa return to the kitchen. Lights dim in the
kitchen except a small spot on the clock over the
door which advances one hour. Lights come up
and Reesa is in the kitchen washing dishes. The
sun is beginning to rise.*

REESA
(calls to her mother off stage)
Shouldn't they be back by now?

(The roar of the old truck is heard as it returns and stops quickly outside the back door. Reesa jumps up and opens the door.)

REESA
Daddy, what's wrong?

WARREN
(off stage)
Roo, get your mother. We need blankets, towels. Quick!

(Reesa runs out the back door instead of toward her mother's room. Warren and Luther are dragging a bloody, battered MARVIN between them. His head is loosely wrapped in the shirt Warren wore before he left. Blood is everywhere. Marvin's face is beaten and swollen almost beyond recognition. They push past Reesa into the house.)

WARREN
Stand back now!
(Marvin moans softly and without power. Reesa runs past them and snatches up the items on the kitchen table.)

REESA

Here, Daddy. Put him here.

(They lay Marvin on the kitchen table. Elizabeth rushes in horrified.)

Marvin, you all right?

LUTHER

(yells)

G'wan now, Roo.

(takes a towel from Elizabeth who grabs Reesa by the shoulders and drags her back)

WARREN

Lizbeth!

(places a blanket over Marvin's inert form and lifts the rags around Marvin's head. He looks at Elizabeth and shakes his head almost imperceptibly. Elizabeth pulls Reesa to the living Room.)

ELIZABETH

(falls to her knees hugging Reesa who is struggling to return to the kitchen)

No, Roo! No!

WARREN
(looks at Luther deciding what to do)
> Lizbeth, call Doc Johnson! Tell him we
> have a bad case of Klan fever! Real bad!
> We'll be at his door in ten minutes!

ELIZABETH
(walks shakily to the phone on the wall in the
kitchen. She looks at Marvin, stricken. Reesa
falls to her knees in shock in the living room as
she looks at the scene in the kitchen.)
> Okay. Go. Go!

WARREN
> Damn them! Damn those Klanners to
> hell!

(They get Marvin's body between them and head
out the still open back door. Blood is on the table
and the floor. The old truck is heard leaving
quickly.)

REESA
(runs toward the door to follow. Elizabeth drops
the phone and steps between Reesa and the door)
> Let me go! I wanna go with Marvin! Let
> me go!

ELIZABETH
No, Roo. Don't look. No.

REESA
(cries now ~ sobs)
Marvin. Marvin!

Scene 2

*The McMahon House two days later. The kitchen is
cleaned up and back to normal except for the solemnity
of the house. Warren sits alone at the piano playing
"I'm Just a Poor Wayfaring Stranger". He wears black
pants and a white shirt with a black tie. Reesa enters.*

REESA
Pretty good, Daddy. It sounds how I feel.

WARREN
(stops playing)
I know, Reesa Roo. Me too.

REESA
Your polio arm doesn't seem to bother
you when you play.
(perches on the bench next to her father)

WARREN
Piano saved this arm. It's not as good as
it used to be, but it's still pretty useful.
(He raises his right arm and looks at it.)
Kept this one limber too.
(He shrugs the left.)
Your Grandma Dot came down here and
found me all in splints, and she nearly

tore the doctor's head off. She told him I
needed activity or those muscles would
wither away for sure. As usual, Dot was
right. The doctor still crosses the street
when he sees her coming.
>   (laughs softly)

>   REESA
Did you really catch the polio from a
lake?

>   WARREN
I was wading in Round Lake one day and
came down with the polio the next.
Worst luck possible it was the same year
your mother was pregnant with you,
Reesa. A lot of folks pitched in and
helped ~ even though we were Yankees.
Of course, then Dot came down, and she
put everything straight again.

>   REESA
Daddy, is it true what Dot says about our
Mayflower ancestor, Richard Warren
being called 'The Stranger'?

WARREN

Yes, honey. On *The Mayflower*, the
Pilgrims were called the Saints. Richard
Warren worked for the company that paid
for their trip to the new world. Still, the
Pilgrims referred to the outsiders as The
Strangers.

REESA

When we studied them last fall, Mrs.
Beacham said she never heard of such a
thing.

WARREN

True story, Roo.

REESA

Dot says she's afraid she jinxed you by
naming you after him.

WARREN

Maybe so, Roo. Sometimes I know
exactly how he felt.

REESA

Will the funeral last long?

WARREN

Several hours, I'd guess. There's the
service and burial. Then a gathering at
Luther and Armetta's. After that, there's
a meeting with Reverend Stone and some
of the elders.

REESA

What kind of meeting?

WARREN

We need to discuss our options, Rooster.

REESA

You mean you're going to talk about
finding the man who killed Marvin.

WARREN

The Klan killed Marvin, Roo. The
question is why. And what's to be done
about it.

REESA

But you always said the Klan was nothing
to be afraid of. Just a bunch of good ol'
boys playing boogey-man.

WARREN

(slumps a bit at hearing his reassuring lie ring false)

Like Dot says, we're strangers in a strange land. The Klan's been around here for years ~ mostly pulling pranks. Burning crosses, pestering couples parking at night, picking on Negroes when they get uppity ~ whatever that means. But this week they crossed the line.

REESA

But May Carol's daddy's in the Klan. May Carol says it's nothing but a card club ~ an excuse to play poker. And Armetta works for them in their house!

WARREN

Lord, Roo. It's a complicated mess. I wish we'd known more about it before we bought all this property and...

ELIZABETH

(enters from hallway wearing a black dress which is unzipped down the back. She approaches Warren and turns so he can zip the dress.)
Warren?

(Warren zips the dress)
Roo, make sure you finish up the breakfast dishes before Dot gets in there. If she starts putting things away, it could easily turn into another 'Let's clean out the cupboard' project.

REESA

Dot is terribly partial to cleaning. She almost started on my ears this morning. I told her I just did them. I'll get to the dishes right away.

ELIZABETH

(checks her watch)
We should be going, don't you think?

REESA

Are you sure I can't come, Mama?

ELIZABETH

A funeral is no place for a little girl, Reesa. Stay here and keep Dot company.

WARREN
(picks up the suit jacket that matches his pants.
Calls down the hall)
        We're leaving, Dot.
(to Reesa)
        You lovely ladies try to stay out of
        trouble, okay?
(grins widely)

ELIZABETH
(to Warren)
You look like a pirate.

WARREN
(bows grandly)
        At your service, m'lady.
(they walk to the back door to exit)

ELIZABETH
Bye, Reesa. Be good.
                (exit)

REESA
(Reesa goes starts on dishes. Marvin sits quietly
at the table. He wears his usual dungarees and a
work shirt as he would on any normal day.
Reesa doesn't notice him until he speaks. He is
in relative dark until he speaks. Then light comes
up on Marvin)
Marvin's dead. Gone forever.

MARVIN
Naw, I wouldn't say that 'zactly, Miss
Reesa Roo How Do You Do!

REESA
(runs to him and hugs him tight)
Marvin! Marvin! Is it really you?

MARVIN
Sure it's me! Who you spectin'?

REESA
But Marvin…
(hesitates)
You're dead. Gone forever. Mamma
said so.

MARVIN
Am I, Reesa Rooster?

REESA

Mommy and Daddy are at your funeral.

MARVIN

That's might nice of 'em. They's always
good folks. I'll be sorry to miss 'em.

REESA

But shouldn't you be there, Marvin?

MARVIN

Don't much care for funerals, Roo.
Besides, can't stand to see my Mamma
cry.

REESA

Oh, Marvin. I'm so glad you're back! I
thought it was real. I thought you were
dead. Gone forever.

MARVIN

Well, I am dead, Roo.

REESA

Then, how'd you get here, Marvin?

MARVIN

Rooster, you and me, we friends from
way back. Would you say that's so?

REESA

Yes.

MARVIN

Well, Roo. When your good friend dies,
he ain't really gone. Certainly not
forever.

REESA

He's not?

MARVIN

No, he's not. Reesa, when you remember
me, do you feel me here?
(touches his temple)
And here?
(touches his heart)

REESA

Yes, Marvin. Yes, every time. It feels
like I'm going to break in two.

MARVIN
You can't do that, Roo. I need you.
Need you to find out who did this.

REESA
Me? Don't you know?

MARVIN
Not rightly. That' why I need you.

REESA
But how can you talk to me, Marvin?
How are you here?

MARVIN
I'm all the memories. All the good times
and the fun we had together, Roo. As
long as you have your memories, I'll
never really be gone.

REESA
You won't?

DOT
(enters hallway from a bedroom in back as light
goes black over Marvin. As Reesa walks toward
Dot, Marvin slips away.)
    Reesa, honey. Are you talking to me?

REESA

No, Dot! Look! It's Marvin!
(she grabs Dot's hand and drags her into the
kitchen. Marvin is not there. Reesa is surprised.)

DOT

Honey, things are going to remind you of
Marvin for a long time. I know you're
hurting. We all are. I have an idea.
(she turns and walks down the hall toward her
bedroom)

REESA

(settles on piano bench)
What kind of idea?

DOT

A good idea, I think.
(returns with her purse.)
Let me check my cash on hand first.

REESA

That means a treat!

DOT
(counts money from her purse)
Only if I have enough ~ And I do! I'm
thinking clam chowder might just hit the
spot today. What do you think?

REESA
I haven't had chowder since the last time
you came!

DOT
Only place for chowder is the Lakeview
Inn up in Mount Dora.

REESA
Lakeview Inn!? They have the biggest
hot fudge sundaes in the state!

DOT
Let's take a little drive then, shall we?

REESA
(hugs her)
Oh, Dot! You're the best.

*They exit and lights dim on the house as a small
set is wheeled on in front of the house which
represents the Lakeview Inn. The background is*

*large windows, surrounded by a profusion of
flowers, and looking out over a beautiful blue
lake. It is a bright sunny day. Two booths
(ideally) or tables are on the platform and are
side by side in front of the windows. These
booths are separated by a curtain which hangs
between them. In one booth, there are three men.
One of them is DONNELLY. He sits in the back
corner of the booth, mostly obstructed from view,
and his hat lays beside him, unnoticed. The other
men are JOHN IVEY and MORRIS BELLVIEW,
both Klan members. The are frozen in tableau as
the set comes on stage, and there is no light on
them until they speak. Reesa and Dot enter.*

HOSTESS
(delighted)
Mrs. McMahon! Has it been a year
already?

DOT
Certainly seems that way!

HOSTESS
Your granddaughter is growing like a
weed. She's more like her father every
time I see her. I have a pretty booth by
the window.

                    DOT
That's fine.

                  HOSTESS
Drive down again this season?

                    DOT
Yep. I love that DeSoto.

                  HOSTESS
Me too! I've never seen that color blue
on any other car. One of a kind Ms.
McMahon! One of a kind! Mary Sue'll
take care of you. Good seeing you again!

                    DOT
You too!
(they slide into the booth with Dot on one side
and Reesa on the other. Reesa has her back to
the other booth.)
Your grandfather and I used to winter
across the lake there.
(points)
The first time I brought your father here,
he was just a babe in arms.

MARY SUE
(approaches Reeesa and Dot with huge menus.
She passes them around with a friendly smile.)
        Get you something to drink while you
        look at the menu.

REESA
Coke for me, please!

DOT
Iced tea.

MARY SUE
One coke and one iced tea.
(walks away)

REESA
Is that why Mommy and Daddy bought
the grove here, Dot?

DOT
Probably. Your father has a lot of
pleasant memories of his winters here in
Florida. This was always a peaceful,
happy place, but I guess when you're a
tourist, you never see the truth of a place.
        I never, for the life of me, had any idea…
(shakes her head)

DOT (cont.)
So? Clam chowder or the fried clams this time?

REESA
I think the clams. We can share.

DOT
A wonderful idea!

MARY SUE
(returns with drinks)
One coke and one iced tea. Ready to order?

DOT
I'll have the clam chowder, and this young lady would like your fried clams with French fries.
(light comes up on the other booth as Dot orders and is at full strength when a burst of male laughter is heard from the men sitting there. Dot is stirring her iced tea with a long spoon when she hears the men speak. She freezes.)

JOHN IVEY

(laughs loud and long)

    The hell of it is, they grabbed the wrong
    nigger!

MARY SUE

(Ignores what has been said nearby)

    That all?

DOT

(ice in her eyes)

    For now.

(Mary Sue exits)

MORRIS BELLVIEW

    They cruised the juke joint and saw him ~
    young buck leanin' up against this white
    Caddy with New York plates. Uppity-ass
    burr-head smart-talked Jimmy Sims at his
    garage! They got the bastard. Shut him
    up right quick and headed for a little
    stompin' party at Round Lake.

(sips loudly from his iced tea)

MORRIS BELLVIEW (cont.)
Reed Garnet. Y'all know him? Got there
a little late and half-dead nigger looks up
at him and whimpers, 'Mr. Reed, Mr.
Reed, it's me, Marvin!'
(Morris, John, and Deputy Donnelly laugh while
at the Warren table, Dot stares at Reesa, silently
warning her not to make a sound.)
Well, Reed, he was hoppin' mad. Called
those boys a bunch of morons. Told them
this boy's mamma works in his house and
now what was he gonna do? J.D.
Bowman, y'all know that crazy Apopka
boy just back from Korea? Well, J.D., he
just laughed. Pulled out his pistol and
shot that nigger boy in the head.
'Problem solved', he told Reed.
(Donnelly and John Ivey laugh again.)

JOHN IVEY
I saw old Reed at the Zellwood Café.
Said I hoped he wasn't too broke up about
it. It's good t' kill a nigger every once in
a while. Keeps the rest of 'em in line.
(They nod and chuckle)

DONNELLY
(Mary Sue approaches the table. She is as
friendly to the men as she is to Dot and Reesa.)
Way I look at it, one less nigger makes
the world a cleaner place. Mary Sue,
honey, it's my turn to buy these ol' boys
their pie and coffee.

MARY SUE
I was just bringing the bill. Here ya go.

(He hands her a five dollar bill, and she makes
change at the table. Reesa and Dot continue to
sit frozen, listening in horror. Reesa is nearly
overcome by tears, but she refuses to move, and
merely wipes her eye on her shoulder while she
listens.)

MARY SUE
Here's your change.

DONNELLY
Keep that, honey!
(he grins)
See ya tomorrow.

MARY SUE
Thank ya kindly. You boys be good now.

(She backs up and walks toward the kitchen as
the men rise from the booth.)

                    JOHN IVEY
            Now you're starting to sound like my
            wife, Mary Sue!
(Slowly the men stand, hitch up their pants, and
start to walk out the door, past Reesa and Dot
who they don't even notice. The men talk as
they head to the door.)

                  MORRIS BELLVIEW
            Heading to the hardware store for barbed
            wire for that back fence.

                    JOHN IVEY
            What happened to the old one?

                  MORRIS BELLVIEW
            Just got old and came down, I reckon.
(The last man out, Deputy Donnelly, is wearing
an official Orange County Deputy Sheriff's
uniform. He pulls his hat out of the booth and
places it on his head. Reesa and Dot look at each
other horrified as they realize who they've just
heard speaking.)

DONNELLY
Happens to the best of us.

MARY SUE
(Mary Sue returns with a large tray of food which she distributes efficiently)
Awful quiet today!
(no one responds)
I hope y'all saved room for sundaes.
(She walks away without waiting for a response.)

DOT
Reesa, not one word until we're in the car.
(lights out)

Scene 3

(In the kitchen at the house, Reesa and her family
are huddled around the kitchen table as Dot
recounts her story to Elizabeth and Warren, who
still wear their funeral clothes. Elizabeth holds a
handkerchief which she twists occasionally.
They all sit spellbound as Dot stands at the head
of the table and speaks)

DOT
(livid)
To hear that idiot talk about Marvin like
the boy was an animal, a dog to be put out
of his misery… I swear I could have
killed him with my bare hands! I want
you to call the constable and get him over
here now. He's going to go arrest those
men today! Right this minute!

WARREN
The constable's a card-carrying member
of the Klan! His standard line with any
crime against a colored person is, 'We'll
look into it.' But he never does.

DOT
You mean he hasn't even opened a case?

WARREN

Probably not.

DOT

Can't you call the sheriff or one of the
county commissioners?

WARREN

Mom, the sheriff, the commissioners,
even the Apopka Chief of Police ~ they're
all Klan members! Even the goddamn
Governor, Fuller Warren is one of them!

DOT

Governor Warren! That's one Warren
who's no possible relation to us!

(paces)

The Klan owns this state like Capone
owned Chicago! He owned the city, the
county, the state, but…

(brilliant idea as she locks eyes with Warren)

…you remember how they got rid of him!

REESA

We learned about him in history. Mrs.
Hudson said the FBI caught Al Capone!

WARREN

The FBI? Interesting… I don't know
how Mr. Hoover feels about the Klan, but
I know he's no fan of cold-blooded
killing. We could try to contact him. But
how? We can't call. We'd never get
through. Besides…

ELIZABETH
(quietly)
Maybelle…

DOT

What?

ELIZABETH
(louder)
Maybelle. She shares our party line.

WARREN

Lizbeth's right. Maybelle would listen on
the line and blab it all over town! None
of us would be safe.

REESA

What about a letter?

ELIZABETH
Maybelle just happens to be our
postmistress too.

WARREN
If the FBI ever wrote back, the return
address would be a dead giveaway. It'd
be all over town before we ever got the
letter.

DOT
How did you manage to get so lucky as to
share a party line and your mail delivery
with the town busybody?

ELIZABETH
Maybe we shouldn't get involved,
Warren.

REESA
(ignores Elizabeth)
We *could* send a registered letter from
downtown Orlando and use Grandma
Dot's return address in LaGrange.

DOT

(delighted)

Of course! Blanche would forward it
here inside the packet she sends me each
week!

WARREN

It could work!

DOT

It will work! Even Maybelle can't see
inside Blanche's packets!

ELIZABETH

If you're sure you want to risk it.
Blanche'll be our trump card.

WARREN

That's the plan then.
(stands and goes to living room where he pulls
out an old typewriter. He puts three sheets of
paper with carbon papers in between into the
typewriter.)

ELIZABETH
(Wanders to the doorway between the kitchen
and living room)
    We going to tell Luther and Armetta?

WARREN
    Not yet. Let's not get their hopes up until
    we know something definite.

DOT
(walks to refrigerator)
    Lizbeth, I believe I owe this girl some ice
    cream.
(opens the freezer and pulls out a carton.)
    Got any fudge sauce?

Scene 4

(The beauty shop set is brought on stage in front
of the house. If possible, an old water fountain
should be secured to the outside wall of the set.
Over the water fountain hangs a hand-lettered
sign which reads "Whites Only".

Mz. Lillian and Miss Iris are working. Dot sits in
the chair with Mz. Lillian working on her nails.
She is covered by a large plastic cape which
avoids the need for the actress to change costume
here. Reesa sits off to one side, paging through a
magazine and listening surreptitiously to the
conversation. She has a new shirt on or may be
wearing a dress. Iris is unpacking a box of hair
care products and sweeping up around the shop.)

>MZ. LILLIAN
>(to Iris)
>Well, Vivan Brass, the deacon's wife told
>me the Apopka Klanners are all a little
>trigger happy right now because of that
>Lake County business.

>REESA
>What Lake County Business?

IRIS
Didn't you hear?

MZ. LILLIAN
It was all over the news when it
happened!

DOT
I've only been here a few weeks, and
what with Marvin's murder and all...

IRIS
Shame about that.

MZ. LILLIAN
Now, Iris, you don't know what that boy
did. Chances are he had it comin'.
Anyhow, well, this business in Lake
County is just horrible. Seems about a
year ago, a white couple was drivin'
home after dark, and their car broke down
somewhere on a back country road.

IRIS
Four black boys stopped and offered them
a ride to the gas station.

MZ. LILLIAN

Now, you tellin' this, Iris, or am I?
Apparently, the husband didn't want to
leave the car alone out there, so the wife
went with them for help. Alone.

IRIS

Though what white woman in her right
mind would get in a car with four
Negroes, I want to know!

REESA

I ride with our pickers out to the grove.

MZ. LILLIAN

Your folks'll put a stop to that soon
enough. Anyhow, the woman didn't
come back, but next morning the husband
found her talkin' to the man at the gas
station. She told the husband she'd been
kidnapped, and...
(glances at Reesa then continues)
Bothered.

DOT

Bothered?

MZ. LILLIAN
I don't want to be indiscreet in front of
the child, but you know, Ma'am.
Bothered.

DOT
Oh, bothered. Oh, oh, that's awful!

MZ. LILLIAN
Sure was! Well, the white men in
Groveland got all riled up, and Sheriff
Willis McCall deputized the whole bunch
into a posse. They searched the
countryside for these men the papers were
calling "The Groveland Four".

REESA
I heard about them! Daddy read it in the
paper.

MZ. LILLIAN
One of those coloreds was shot tryin' to
escape, but the other three were caught
and stood trial together. The jury found
them guilty. The two oldest will get the
chair. The other one was only fifteen, so
he got life in prison.

DOT

Do you happen to remember who was on the jury?

MZ. LILLIAN

On the jury?

DOT

Were they whites or coloreds?

MZ. LILLIAN

Coloreds may be votin' now, Mz. McMahon, but here in Florida, we only have white men on our juries. Well, the N double A CP got wind of it, and their New York attorney, Mr. Thurgood Marshall, said the trial was unfair and filed an appeal. The *Florida* Supreme Court said the trial was fine, but Mr. Marshall took his story all the way to the *U.S.* Supreme Court. They said the trial wasn't fair on account of the jury being white and the local paper getting people all riled up about it.

IRIS
(grabs a magazine off the pile next to Reesa)
Here! Here's that article they wrote about
it in Time Magazine! Says here, "This is
one of the best examples of one of the
worst menaces to American justice I've
ever seen." Ain't that somethin'?

MZ. LILLIAN
So, now there's gonna be a trial for the
two men on death row. And don't you
bet Sheriff Willis McCAll ain't fit to be
tied about that!

IRIS
Isn't he some big, high muckety-muck
with the Klan up in Lake County?

MZ. LILLIAN
Wouldn't surprise me a bit! I know some
folks don't think much of the Klan, but as
a woman, I have to say I sleep better
knowin' the Klan's around to keep the
Nigras from goin' wild. Afterall, they're
a dark danger to southern womanhood.
(pause)

Reesa, your family comin' to the church
picnic this weekend? I just love your
Mamma's Fruit Cocktail Cake.

(Lights dim and go out)

Scene 5

(Easter night at the McMahon house. Reesa stands in the kitchen with Elizabeth. They are peeling Easter eggs out of a basket and placing the hard boiled eggs in a bowl on the kitchen table. It is dark outside when a tap is heard at the door.)

ELIZABETH

Come in!

LUTHER

Evenin', MizLibeth. Howdy doo, Reesa Roo. Y'all have a nice Easter? Did Warren use "Up From the Grave He Arose"?

REESA

Doesn't he always?

LUTHER

When you direct a church choir like your Daddy and me, Roo, you stick with what the people like!

REESA
Did you use that song too, Luther?

LUTHER
Every year, Roo!

ELIZABETH
Our Easter was fine. How about you?

LUTHER
Good as could be. All things
considered…

ELIZABETH
Armetta do her solo?

LUTHER
Ah wish you coulda heard her. It was
touched by God! The whole church
house was lifted up. Lifted right up!

ELIZABETH
Wish we could have been there. Please
tell Armetta I'm thinking of her.
(lays a hand on his forearm as she speaks to
Reesa)
Reesa, show Luther in to Daddy, please.

WARREN

(looks up from his newspaper as they enter. Reesa sits down quietly in a chair and pretends to read as she listens.)

What is it, Luther?

LUTHER

Armetta's plum grief-struck over losing our Marvin. Since it was Klan that kilt him, and Mistuh Reed Garnet's a Klan member, Armetta swears she can't never set foot in they house again. Miz Lucy Garnet's been up to our house with the little girl, crying, 'please come back'. Saying Mistuh Reed had nothin' to do with it. It was Lake County devils kilt our boy. Armetta won't take a listen ~ though she loves that May Carol Garnet like her own. Such a sweet child. But MistaWarren, Armetta's used to workin'. She needs to work! Somethin' to take her mind off funeralizin'. Ah'm wonderin' if you might have some work for her to do.

REESA

(jumps up and comes to Warren's side)

Please, Daddy! Can't Armetta come here?

LUTHER
Oh, not in the house. We know your
Mamma likes to tend her own. Maybe at
the packinghouse ~ cleaning up, clearing
out. Just enough to get by 'til she finds a
new fam'ly to work for.

REESA
Please, Daddy! Please!

WARREN
We don't usually hire help this time of
year, except Robert to sweep a couple
times a week.

REESA
Humpf!

WARREN
But… it has been several seasons since
the showroom had a thorough cleaning.
We could keep Armetta busy for a week
or so ~ maybe two.
(to Reesa)
Does that work for you?

REESA
Yes, Daddy! Thank you!

LUTHER

Bless you, MistaWarren. Thank you.
Can she start tomorrow?

WARREN

Eight o'clock. Before it gets too hot.

LUTHER

They's somethin' else.
(Warren nods, encouraging him to continue)
        I had a visit from Mistuh Harry T. Moore.
        You know who he is?

REESA

No. Who is he?

WARREN

Leads the N double A CP over in Brevard
County, doesn't he? Helped the Negro
teachers get better pay?

LUTHER

That's him. 'Cept he's the state leader
now. Mr. Moore heard 'bout Marvin and
come to see me and Armetta, askin' what
the authorities been doin' 'bout it. Ah
told him the constable's lookin' into it,
which he said is 'bout like a diamondback

wonderin' where that rattlin' noise is
comin' from.

WARREN
Exactly.

LUTHER
So, Mistuh Harry T. Moore say he talked
to Mistuh Thurgood Marshall 'bout what
happened. You know him? Head lawyer
for the N double A CP in New York City.

WARREN
Know *of* him.

LUTHER
Mistuh Moore said since we was together
when we found Marvin, Mistuh Marshall
be wantin' to talk to you, MistaWarren.
Mistuh Moore say Ah need to ask if
you'd be willin' to talk to them.

WARREN
Of course, Luther. I'd welcome the
chance to talk to either of them.

LUTHER

Mistuh Moore say Mistuh Marshall been
a good friend of the coloreds in Florida.
He say Mistuh Marshall has a big friend
in Washington, D.C. might be able to get
the local authorities to pay more attention
to this.

WARREN

I'll help any way I can.

LUTHER
(emotional)
The hang of it is, Jerry Tee heard some of
those ol' Crackers talkin' at the gas
station. They say the Klan wasn't even
after Marvin. They just confused him
with somebody else in a white Cadillac
with New York plates.

WARREN
(quietly as he looks at Reesa)
I heard that too.

LUTHER

(pulls out a large handkerchief and blows his
nose)

> MistaWarren, the Klan done kilt our boy
> for nothin'.

WARREN

> I know, Luther. I can't even begin to tell
> you how bad I feel about it.

REESA

(looks at floor)

> Me too, Luther.

(wanders back to her seat and picks up her book)

LUTHER

> Thank you. Ah couldn't tell Armetta
> 'bout that, and Ah warned Jerry Tee to be
> muffle-jawed in her direction. Her
> heart's done broke enough already. Ah
> 'pologize for spoilin' your evenin'.

WARREN

> No apologies, Luther. Armetta's isn't the
> only heart that's hurting around here.

(looks at Reesa who's been pretending to do
homework.)

Probably time for you to get to bed,
Reesa. School tomorrow.

REESA
(Rises reluctantly and gives her father a hug)
Guess so. Good night, Daddy. Night,
Luther.

LUTHER
G'night Rooster! Sleep tight. Don't let
the bed bugs bite!

REESA
I won't, Luther!

(Reesa exits to her bedroom. She turns on the
small lamp there, pulls her nightgown over her
head, and shrugs out of her other clothes from
beneath the nightgown. This action occurs as the
discussion between Luther and Warren continues.
When she's ready for bed, she brushes her hair
until her cue.)

LUTHER
Folks in The Quarters are scared outta
their wits. Most of 'em grabbin' they
children off the street at the least li'l noise
or a motor-by of a white man's truck.

The chil'ren are havin' night terrors too.
Hardly a night goes by that Ah don't hear
a couple of 'em, up and down the way,
wakin' up screamin' in they beds.

WARREN
These people must be stopped! There has
to be a way!

LUTHER
Ah wish they was, MistaWarren. Ah
sincerely wish they was.

(Lights dim on living room as Reesa finishes
brushing her hair in the bedroom. She throws
herself onto the bed.)

REESA
(upset)
Marvin's dead. Gone forever! Marvin's
dead. Gone forever!

(Marvin appears in the dark. It is easiest if he
slips unnoticed out of Reesa's closet, and leans
there against the door jamb until he speaks.)

MARVIN

Now, Rooter-Tooter-Where's-Yo-
Scooter, I keep tellin' you that ain't so!

REESA

(rises and grabs him in a hug)
You're back! I know who did it, Marvin!
I know who killed you!

MARVIN

Who, Reesa Roo? Who was it?

REESA

Well, Daddy say the Klan killed you, but
Dot and I heard some Klanners say J.D.
Bowman shot you in the head.

MARVIN

J.D. Bowman, eh?

REESA

You going to get him, Marvin? You
going to get even?

MARVIN

Why should I? The constable's gonna
take care of the justice. I just wanted to
know, Roo.

REESA

But there's no case. The constable turned his back. He's a Klanner too, Marvin.

MARVIN

Then, I guess I'll have to wait for divine justice, Rooster.

REESA

No, Marvin. That's not good enough!

MARVIN

The Lord hisself not good enough! Good enough for me, I reckon.

REESA

That's not what I meant…

MARVIN

I know what you mean, Reesa. I know. Hey, weren't I gonna teach you proper dancin' this year for yo' birthday?

REESA

You said you would…

MARVIN

Come on then. Dry them tears. Ain't no
good dancing done when you're cryin'.
Now, take my hand here.

REESA

Like this?

MARVIN

Yes'm. Now put your other hand here.

REESA

Okay. Marvin, if you're not real, how
can you teach me to dance?

MARVIN

I done tol' you, Roo. I'm your memories
of me. You saw me dance lotsa times.
Think back on it.

REESA

I'll try, Marvin. I'll try.

MARVIN

Now, Ah count, and you just listen to the
beat. That's the key, Rooster. Just listen.
One, two, three. One two, three.

(they start to dance together in a stilting, starting, stopping waltz. Suddenly it becomes smooth and beautiful, and the sound of music starts lightly and gets louder. Suddenly Reesas stops ~ the music along with her.)

                    REESA
          Marvin, I won't let the Klan win! I
          won't! Whatever it takes, I'll make sure
          they pay!

                    MARVIN
          Ain't no beating the Klan, Reesa. Now
          you gone and broke my concentration.
          Start again. One, two, three. One, two,
          three…
(Music returns as they dance out. The lights and music fade.)

Scene 6

A bright, sunny summer morning. The citrus tree
outside the house no longer has pretty blossoms.
The tree looks green and leafy all over.
Breakfast for one sits on the table, waiting for
Reesa. She enters, dressed for the day and sits at
the place mat and bowl and starts to eat.

Elizabeth enters through the back door wearing
work clothes. She is followed by Armetta.

ELIZABETH
See, Armetta, I told you she'd be up by
now. Good morning, Reesa.

REESA
Morning, Mamma. Thanks for the
oatmeal.

ELIZABETH
You're welcome. Armetta wanted to see
you. She came to help in the
packinghouse today. She brought you
something.

(Armetta carries a plate covered with a large, clean napkin. She sets this on the counter as she talks to Reesa)

REESA
(shyly)
Hey, Armetta.

ARMETTA
Reesa Roo!
(Hugs Reesa then steps back to look at her.)
Gotta get a look at you! Girl! You weren't no bigger that a minute when you was born... You're a pretty half-hour now!

REESA
(uncertain for a moment. Then she falls weeping into Armetta's warm hug)
Oh, Armetta! Marvin's dead! Gone forever!

ARMETTA
Oh, chil', mah boy loved you like his own sister.

REESA
(cries)
He was my best friend. He was the best
friend in the whole world, and… and…
Everything's all upside down without
him!

ARMETTA
(holds Reesa close until she's done crying. Then
she pushes her back just enough to look into her
face as she speaks.)
Reesa, lemme tell you somethin'. When
Ah was 'bout your age, Ah lost someone
too. My old granmamma tol' me
somethin' Ah've nevea forgot. God is the
potter, she said, and we clay in his hands
~ soft and weak ~ which don't do at all.
It's our time in the fire, don't ya see,
makes us strong ~ shows us His purpose.
Without that, we couldn't hold water.
Y'understand?
(Reesa nods)
God has His plans, honey, for all of us ~
you, Marvin, me, your mamma and
daddy, everybody. And, He gotta prepare
us. Time in the fire don't burn us, y'see.
It helps us be ready for whatever's ahead.

REESA

But Marvin's gone forever!

ARMETTA

His work was done, Reesa. His time
come.

REESA

But why couldn't he just die natural?
Why'd it have to be so awful?

ARMETTA

Oh, chil', there's no explainin' the
meanness in this world. But there's
goodness here too. You can't lose sight
of that. Hold on to it. It's the goodness
gets us through.

REESA

Do you.,. really believe we'll see Marvin
again? Up there, I mean?
                    (points to heaven)

ARMETTA

Ah do, chil'. Ah do. In the meantime…
(reaches for the covered plate)
          Ah brought you some snicker doodles,
          and since Robert traipsed of to O'lando

with your daddy, Ah speck you get the
whole plate to your own self.

REESA

Snicker doodles?
(hugs her tight again)
Thank you, Armetta. Thank you for
everything.

ARMETTA

Have some cookies, girl. Ah gotta get
myself back to work.

(There's a knock at the back door. LUCY
GARNET stands with her perfect hair and
expensive clothes.)

ELIZABETH

Now, who could that be? We'll never
finish cleaning out the showroom.
(opens the door)
Lucy? Well... Can I help you?

LUCY

I was hopin' to speak with Armetta. I
heard she was workin' for you now.
Would you mind, Elizabeth? It won't
take a minute.

ELIZABETH
(not wanting to answer for Armetta)
Armetta?

ARMETTA
Ah don't know Mz. Lucy. I already tol'
you everything there is to say.

LUCY
Armetta, Please?

ELIZABETH
I was just going back across the way. I
have to get back to the inventory. Reesa,
don't you have dusting in the living
room?

REESA
(takes the hint and heads to the living room
where she pretends to dust for a bit, then settles
down by the kitchen wall to listen in)
Yes, Ma'am.

ELIZABETH
Armetta, I'll be just out back if you need
me.
(Elizabeth exits)

ARMETTA
Thank you, MizLizbeth.

LUCY
(stands in her high heels)
Armetta, I'm about to go out of my mind.
May Carol can't sleep, won't eat, won't
hardly do a thing 'cause of missin' you.
During the day, that girl's like a ghost,
wanderin' room to room. Every night,
she just cries and cries. What can I say?
What can I do to get you to come back to
us?

ARMETTA
Mz. Lucy, you know this has nothin' to
do with you and that chil'.

LUCY
Yes, and you know Reed had nothin' to
do with Marvin's death!

ARMETTA
No, Ma'am. Ah can't know that. Ah'm
not sayin' Mistuh Reed pulled the trigger
or nothin' like that. But Ah knows it was
the Klan kilt Marvin, and Mistuh Reed's a
member of the Klan!

LUCY

But, Armetta, there's three different Klan
dens around here. Reed's is just a card
club ~ a bunch of overgrown boys playin'
poker!

ARMETTA

Mz. Lucy, I can't. Ah just can't feature
comin' back to your house. Cookin' and
cleanin', and puttin' clothes in the closet,
seein' that white robe hangin' there.

LUCY

I could make him keep the robe at his
mother's house. I could bring him
around, and he'd swear on the family
Bible he had nothin' to do with this.
Reed already told me he'd do it if it
would get you to come back.

ARMETTA

Ah'm sorry, Mz. Lucy...

LUCY

Armetta, don't you see I'm beggin' you
here?

ARMETTA

Ah'm as sorry as Ah can be. Ah'm sorry
for you and Ah'm sorry for Miss May
Carol, and Ah'm sorry that my Marvin
lies rottin' in his grave at age nineteen
with cuts all over his body and a bullet
hole in his head. Ah could never, ever
again work in the house of a Klan
member!

LUCY
(not wanting to believe, steps backward)
So, you workin' permanent for Warren
and Lizbeth now?

ARMETTA

This just temporary ~ cleaning mostly and
gettin' things ready for the summer
season.

LUCY

Then what?

ARMETTA

Ah hopes to find another family to work
for.

LUCY

In Apopka?

ARMETTA

Yes. Here or Zellwood. It don't matter.
Ah'll find somethin' someplace.

LUCY

I'm sure you will, Armetta. I'm sorry we
couldn't straighten this out.

ARMETTA

Marvin's killin' is somethin' won't ever
be straightened out, Mz. Lucy.

LUCY

Goodbye, Armetta. May Carol asked me
to say 'hey' for her.

ARMETTA

That chil's an angel. Tell her Ah said
she'll always be a precious li'l angel to
me.

LUCY

I, uh... I uh... don't suppose I could get
your snicker doodle recipe. For May
Carol. She asked me to ask.

ARMETTA

You know I do it all outta mah head, but
Ah'll try. If Ah can figure out the
measures, Ah'll write them down and
send 'em on to you.

LUCY

(reaches for the back door handle)
Thank you, Armetta. We'll watch for it.
(Lucy exits)

ARMETTA

(peaks around the corner of the wall where she
knows she will find Reesa listening)
Reesa?

REESA

(stands embarrassed, and enters kitchen)
Yes?

ARMETTA

When you finish them cookies, just bring
the plate and all back to the
packinghouse. I'll be there all week.
(reaches for the door)
Suppose you could help me figure out the
measures I use to make them cookies?

REESA

Yes'm.

ARMETTA

Then, next time we'll do it together. Don't forget your dustin', Roo. Don't want to leave extra work for Dot or your mamma.

REESA

No. I'll wash the plate before I bring it back too.

ARMETTA

See you soon, Rooster.
(exits as Reesa takes a cookie from the plate and watches her leave.)

REESA

(to Armetta as she watches her leave)
Wish I could tell you about the letter to Mr. Hoover, Armetta. Wish I could tell you we're trying to do something! Daddy was right though. Good thing we didn't tell since Mr. Hoover doesn't seem to care either. Here I thought he'd write to Dot right away, but it's been months and nothing! It's not right! It's just not right!

Scene 7

Nightfall in the McMahon home. Dot, Elizabeth,
and Reesa sit at the kitchen table playing cards.
Elizabeth is a fine card player, and she is
teaching Dot and Reesa to play. Warren sits in
the living room reading his paper.

ELIZABETH
Remember, Reesa, if you play the two or
the jack, you freeze the pile.

REESA
Then I have to have a pair to pick up the
top card, right?

DOT
Very good! Chip off the old block, eh,
Elizabeth?

REESA
Did you get your package from Miss
Blanche today, Dot?

DOT
Yes, it came. Still no word. I don't see
how the head of the FBI could ignore a
cold-blooded murder for two months!

ELIZABETH
Maybe he's busy.

DOT
That's why he has agents.

(A knock at the door stops the conversation cold.)

ELIZABETH
Who is it?

LUTHER
Me, MizLizbeth. Luther.

ELIZABETH
(rises and opens the door)
Luther, come on in.

LUTHER
Evenin', Ma'am. Roo. Y'all finished supper?

REESA
Yessir, we have.

LUTHER

Ah brought a couple people to meet
MistaWarren.

ELIZABETH

Please, come in.
(HARRY T. MOORE and THURGOOD
MARSHALL follow Luther into the kitchen.
Elizabeth raises her voice to call Warren.)
Warren, you have company.
(He rises and folds his paper. Walks to the
kitchen)

LUTHER

Ah'd like you t'meet Mistuh Thurgood
Marshall and Mistuh Harry T. Moore.

ELIZABETH

(clears away the card game)
Gentlemen, welcome. Please meet my
mother-in-law, Mrs. Dorothy McMahon.

DOT

(stands)
How do you do?

ELIZABETH

And this is Marie Louise.

HARRY
Also known as Reesa, I hear.

REESA
Pleased to meet you.

ELIZABETH
(indicating Warren as he comes into the kitchen)
And my husband, Warren McMahon.
(shake hands all around)

THURGOOD
It's a pleasure to meet you all.

DOT
You're a long way from home, Mr.
Marshall.

ELIZABETH
(Elizabeth indicates seats at the table, and all sit
down.)
Please, have a seat.

THURGOOD
Thank you, ma'am. I've had business at
the Lake County courthouse all week.
Spent today with Harry registering voters.
Heading home tonight.

LUTHER
(pulls out a white card)
Lookee here! Says Ah'm a duly
registered voter in the County of Orange,
State of Florida. Come next spring, Ah
get to vote in the primary election. After
that, Ah'll help pick the next President of
the United States.

REESA
Haven't you voted before?

LUTHER
Nope.

HARRY
Orange County's been a little slow giving
us the vote, but thanks to Mr. Marshall
here, we're back in the registration
business.

DOT
Good Lord, that amendment passed,
what? Twenty years ago?

THURGOOD

Thirty, actually. But I doubt you need me
to tell you the pace down here's a bit
behind the rest of the country.

ELIZABETH
(to Harry)
How's registration coming?

HARRY

Pretty good so far.

THURGOOD

Harry's being modest. Before he got
involved, less than four percent of the
Negroes in this state were registered.
Now, we're up to nearly thirty percent,
which is twice the level of any other
southern state.

ELIZABETH

Good for you! I'm sure it hasn't been
easy.

HARRY

Ma'am, I need to get Mr. Marshall to the
airport in about two hours. Would it be
all right if we had a word with Mr.
McMahon, alone.

ELIZABETH

Of course, Reesa, go find your
homework.

REESA

But, Mamma…

ELIZABETH

No buts. This is an adult conversation.
Go.

REESA

Daddy?

WARREN

Better do as your Mamma says, Rooster.

(Reesa leaves reluctantly for the living room.
When she's sure the adults are busy in their
conversation, she sneaks over to the wall, and
sinks down to listen.)

THURGOOD

Mr. McMahon…

WARREN

Please, call me Warren.

THURGOOD

We're starting a file on what happened to
Marvin Cully. I'd like to hear your story
and that of your mother.

WARREN

If you'll wait just a minute, I have my
notes in my office.
(he goes through the living room and down the
hall. He sees Reesa behind the wall and stops
briefly, nods, and walks past as though she
wasn't there. He goes into a room and quickly
returns to the kitchen)

THURGOOD

Of course.

ELIZABETH

Please, gentlemen, would you like some
iced tea?

HARRY

Please don't go to any trouble.

ELIZABETH

No trouble at all.

(she goes about the kitchen pouring tea, getting
the sugar bowl, and cutting lemons. She places a
glass in front of Thurgood, Harry, and Warren
when he returns)

WARREN

(returns to kitchen ~ again passing Reesa and
saying nothing. He smiles at her tenacity.)
    Sorry to keep you waiting.
(Holds up a file folder)
        What I have here are four documents.
        The first is the notes I made on Thursday,
        March eleventh, the day Luther and I
        found Marvin on Round Lake Road.
        Except for poor Marvin, it looked pretty
        much like the scene of a party ~ beer
        cans, cigarette butts, a couple of broken
        branches on some of the orange trees, lots
        of tire tracks...
(hands a sheet to Thurgood Marshall.)

HARRY

How'd you know to go to this place?

LUTHER
Everybody knows where the Apopka
Klan takes people…

WARREN
If we hadn't found him there, we'd have
checked the Ocoee Klan's stomping
grounds off Winter Garden Road.

THURGOOD
Harry, can you find out who owns these
properties?

WARREN
Oh, I can tell you that. Emmett
Casselton. He's a big citrus man around
here and longtime Klan member.

THURGOOD
Good. What else do you have?

WARREN
(hands page to Thurgood)
These are the doctor's notes on Marvin's
condition when we brought him in. I've
called the coroner for his report, but I
have a feeling he isn't planning to file
one.

(Thurgood Marshall reads the paper Warren
hands him)

THURGOOD
Another Klanner?

WARREN
Sadly, yes. Here's a transcript of a
conversation my mother and Reesa heard
at the Lakeview Inn, Saturday, March
thirteenth. My mother and I sat down
afterwards. She dictated. I typed. As
you can see, I'm not the world's best
typist.
(passes another page to Thurgood Marshall)

THURGOOD
Did you get a look at this deputy, ma'am?

DOT
Unfortunately, only from the back. He
was a burly man ~ about your size with
big brown freckles all over the back of his
neck and hands. Big-boned too. I'd
guess Irish descent.

THURGOOD

And the waitress? Can you remember her
name?

DOT

No. I'm sorry.

REESA

(bursts out with it as she leans around the
doorway from the other room)
Mary Sue!
(she has the good grace to be embarrassed at her
eavesdropping before she continues)
She had a curly pin on her uniform that
said, 'Mary Sue' plain as day! And that's
what the deputy called her when he asked
for the check.

THURGOOD

You're a very observant young lady.
Anything else?

REESA

(steps into the kitchen, just a bit)
The other two men wore grove boots like
Daddy's. One was tall and real skinny,
stooped like Ichabod Crane. The other

was older with dark hair like Mama and a
big bald spot in the back.

DOT
That's right, Reesa. I'd forgotten.

THURGOOD
Any other details?

REESA
The deputy's gun had a fancy handle.

THURGOOD
What do you mean 'fancy'?

REESA
It was white like the inside of a shell.

THURGOOD
Like a pearl?

REESA
Yes. Like that. And carved maybe.

THURGOOD
Donnelly. Deputy Earl the Pearl
Donnelly. It figures.

WARREN

Roo, you've been a big help.
(hidden in this statement is a warning for Reesa
to leave the room. She reluctantly returns to her
listening post behind the wall.)

THURGOOD

(indicates the paper)
Warren, do you know these people your
mother mentioned here?

WARREN

I know Reed Garnet. But I'm sure
Armetta can tell you more about him than
I can.

THURGOOD

Yes, she filled us in.

WARREN

J.D. Bowman's another story. I know his
father. The old man's a loudmouthed
bigot, worked for Emmet Casselton for
years. Has a grove of his own, but since
most of the local pickers won't work for
him, Bowman brings in migrant labor
instead. I don't know J.D. personally, but
he has a reputation for being a wild hare ~

a real chip of the old block. I don't doubt
for a minute what my mother heard is
exactly what happened. This last is a
copy of a registered letter I sent J. Edgar
Hoover in March.

HARRY

Heard anything back?

WARREN

Not a word.

THURGOOD

Don't surprise me. The director's had his
hands full. Plus, this situation's a little
tricky. Here in Florida, murder's a state
crime. If local lawmen choose not to act,
the feds have to be creative. Otherwise
they lack the authority to get involved. If
you would Warren, I'd like a copy of all
this.

WARREN

Everything was typed with carbons in
triplicate. Take whatever you need.

THURGOOD

Warren, how would you compare the
Orange County Klan to the group I'm
dealing with in Lake County?

WARREN

Well, first, there's the Lake County
sheriff. Willis McCall is a racist son of a
bitch. Excuse me, ladies. And his
deputies are pond scum.

THURGOOD

I have to agree with your assessment on
both counts.

WARREN

Not that our sheriff's much better, but
he's a lot less arrogant. The second thing
is, there are three different Klans in
Orange County. I don't know much
about the one in Orlando, except they
seem to have the good sense to leave the
folks in Eatonville alone. There's another
Klan in Ocoee and Winter Garden, and
that crowd's a lot like the one in Lake
County.

REESA

(bursts in again)
Tell him about the signs, Daddy!

THURGOOD

What signs?

LUTHER

You mean the ones in Ocoee?

THURGOOD

What signs, Luther?

LUTHER

Drivin' in and outta town, they's signs on
both sides sayin' 'Nigger ~ If you can
read this: Don't let the sun set on your
head in Ocoee.'

THURGOOD

Harry, make a note.

WARREN

The Apopka Klan's a little different. The
names I know read like the town register.
Most of the oldest families are involved.
Their grandfathers brought the Klan with
them from Georgia and the Carolinas.

The fathers are pretty quiet, but the
sons… Well, before the war, they mostly
pulled college-boy pranks on young
couples parked in cars and on old
coloreds ~ just to scare them. Now,
they're men, most of them veterans with
experience killing.

> (silence)

THURGOOD
(clears his throat)

Warren, Luther said you'd be a big help,
and he was right. I can't make any
promises. The problem is the state's
jurisdiction and the lack of hard evidence.
If the coroner removed the bullet, and if
the bullet happened to match J.D.
Bowman's gun…

REESA
How will you know if it matches?

HARRY MOORE
First, we have to have the bullet.

WARREN
I have a feeling that bullet's long gone.

THURGOOD
Well, we'll see what we can do.

WARREN
Marvin was a good friend. Not just to me
and Lizbeth but to Reesa. We'll do
whatever we can to help.

(All stand and shake hands. Harry singles out
Reesa)

HARRY
Thank you for all the information, Reesa,
(nods to Elizabeth)
and for opening your home to our little
meeting, ma'am.

REESA
I just want someone to help Marvin.

HARRY
Marvin's beyond help now, child, but
we'll do the best we can!

THURGOOD
(Thurgood Marshall opens the back door to
leave)
> Yes, thank you, Reesa. I've got a lot to
> think about on the trip back to New York.

WARREN
Good night. Safe journey. See you in the
morning, Luther.

LUTHER
Good night.

REESA
(jumps up and swings her fist in victory)
> Now, we're getting somewhere!

ELIZABETH
I don't know…

REESA
Well, they may not be Dick Tracy and
Sam Spade, but since nobody else seems
to care a whit about Marvin, they're all
we've got!

ELIZABETH
(shocked at Reesa's language)
        Reesa!

(Dot and Warren look away or cover their smile
of pride at Reesa'a outburst.)

(End Act I)

ACT II

Scene 1

Reesa, Elizabeth, Dot, Luther, Armetta, and
Warren sit in the living room on a hot summer
afternoon. There are balloons in the kitchen and
a pretty birthday cake, but everyone is crowded
around the radio.

RADIO ANNOUNCER

After the huge bombing at Carver
Village, a Negro housing development in
Miami last month, and the bombing of the
Miami Jewish Community Center earlier
this week, this latest blast at St. Stephen's
Catholic Church today has South Florida
residents deeply concerned. No group
has claimed responsibility for the
bombings, but Florida leaders of the KKK
openly declared war on the N double A
CP, B'Nai Brith, and the Catholic Church
just last month as they said these were
'Hate Groups' intent on quote destroying
our way of life. End quote.

DOT
First the coloreds, then the Jews, and now
the Catholics! It has to be the Klan!

WARREN
It certainly fits their holy trinity of hate.
Nobody else is so obviously ecumenical.

LUTHER
Things that bad in Miami, hafta wonder
how long before the Apopka Klan stirs
things up 'round here again.

DOT
I don't understand why we don't hear
from Mr. Hoover! All this Klan activity
in Florida, you'd think we'd be at the top
of his list!

ARMETTA
Big man like Mr. Hoover ain't gonna care
'bout no colored murder in Apopka.

DOT
Well, maybe it's time I sent my own
letter!

REESA

Daddy, do you think the Klan would do
that here? The bombings, I mean.

WARREN

Hard to say, isn't it? Since nobody's
doing anything to stop what's happening
in Miami, this business could easily get
out of hand. Miami police are looking the
other way, just like ours do. Probably
half Klanners themselves. We know
Thurgood and Harry are doing all they
can, but you'd think the big hotel owners
would be screaming their heads off.

REESA

But, Miami depends on tourism! Won't
the tourists just go someplace else?

WARREN

Once the cancellations start rolling in, the
businesses will be howling for the
governor or somebody to do something.

ELIZABETH

In the meantime?

WARREN
In the meantime, what choice do we have
but to sit tight and keep our heads down.

ARMETTA
I think we should light those birthday
candles. It's still Reesa Roo's birthday,
and we've had enough of the Klan for one
day.

(The sound of a car tearing by the house outside
draws everyone's attention. Warren and Reesa
walk to the window at the front of the house and
look out)

LUTHER
Sounds like newlyweds!

DOT
Too hot for a wedding if you ask me.

LUTHER
You jus' not used to bein' here all
summer, Mz. Dot. You gets used to it.

DOT
I sincerely hope not, but I couldn't leave
until I know my family's safe.

REESA

That's not newlyweds There's four black
men in that car! They look scared!

WARREN

Reesa, get behind the curtain! Look!
Behind the car! In the trucks! Klanners!
(The sound of first one truck and then another
also fly past the house. A loud yell is heard as
one of the trucks pass.)

ELIZABETH

No!
(sinks to the sofa)

WARREN

Two trucks of Klanners, decked out ~
sheets and all in broad daylight! They're
waving guns!
(a gunshot is heard)

LUTHER

(crowds in to see)
Sheets in broad daylight! Ah never seen
it in all my born days.

                    DOT
(looking over their shoulders)
          Look at the trucks. Do you know them?

                  WARREN
          I know some of them all right. J.D.
          Bowman and his boys, and that one...
          Look! Emmett Casselton!
(as he says it Warren eases back from the
window and pulls Reesa with him. He pulls
Luther back as well.)

                    DOT
          Any idea who was in the car?

                  WARREN
          It looked like a rental ~ maybe folks from
          up north.

                 ARMETTA
          I hope they makes it back up north. I'm
          prayin' now they make it anywhere.

                    DOT
          We'll never find out what's going on if
          we just sit here. Reesa, you look like a
          young lady in need of a birthday
          manicure.

REESA

I do?

DOT

Let's have some cake and lemonade.
We'll go visit Mz. Lillian tomorrow for
some beautifying and the latest Klan
news.

ELIZABETH

She's too young for a manicure, Dot.

REESA

Mama!

DOT

Oh, it's just a little paint and polish.
Comes right off! Besides, it's not her
nails we really want. It's the news Mz.
Lillian will be spilling as soon as we get
there.

REESA

I get it. Can I? Please, Mamma? We're
perfectly safe at Mz. Lillian's.

ELIZABETH

Just like your grandmother, aren't you.
Go. Go ahead, you two. But keep a
watchful eye.

DOT

She'll be with me in the DeSoto. No one
would dare chase down the DeSoto!
(They walk toward the kitchen and the cake as
the lights dim on the house. The beauty shop set
returns with Mz. Lillian working on Dot while
Reesa sits with her hands in a bowl having a
manicure with Iris.)

MZ. LILLIAN

So, then I heard it was none other than
that Thurgood Marshall the Klan was
chasing!

IRIS

The attorney from New York?
(pats Reesa's hand dry with a towel and starts to
file her nails)

MZ. LILLIAN

It's his own fault really. He should mind
his own business and stay up north, but
no, he had to come stir things up in Lake

County. Sheriff McCall is none too
happy about that retrial! What'd that
uppity colored lawyer think the Klan was
gonna do ~ welcome him back with open
arms?

                    DOT
Did they get him?

                 MZ. LILLIAN
I heard the Apopka Klan just wanted to
scare him a little on his way to the airport.
They were waiting for him in Zellwood at
the county line. Chased that car all the
way to Orlando but lost him in airport
traffic.

                    DOT
How in the world do you get your
information?

                 MZ. LILLIAN
The girl who does my cleaning is a maid
for Emmett Casselton. She might have
heard a word or two from Emmett. She
told me all about it before choir practice.

REESA
Sally Gibson works for Emmett
Casselton?

MZ. LILLIAN
That she does, honey.

REESA
And she sings in the choir at Luther's
church?

MZ. LILLIAN
She certainly can't sing in the choir at my
church. They have their own service for
the coloreds.

DOT
(looks meaningfully at Reesa)
Isn't that a small world?

IRIS
Ain't it though? You want pink this
time...
(holds up a bottle of nail polish)
Or that pretty red?

DOT
Pink for Reesa. I'll go for the red!

(Lights dim)

Scene 2

(An afternoon in the fall. The citrus tree out
front now bears half-orange half green fruit.
Reesa enters through the back door with her
school books. She finds Thurgood Marshall
talking to her father in the living room.)

                    WARREN
          Don't slam that door. We've got
          company.

                    REESA
          I won't.
(She peaks to see who's with her father. Then
goes to the refrigerator to get a bottle of milk.
Takes a few cookies out of the cookie jar and sits
where she can listen to the conversation.)

                    THURGOOD
          Still no word from the FBI, eh?

                    WARREN
          I knew Florida officials were dirty, but I
          thought Hoover would send help before

now. It's October! Marvin was killed six
months ago!

THURGOOD
Well, could be worse. Could be on your
way with me to tangle with Sheriff Willis
McCall.

WARREN
You got the re-trial for the Groveland
Four. That was certainly a miracle.

THURGOOD
Ackerman, the defense counsel, filed for a
change of venue. Judge Futch is
supposed to rule on it day after tomorrow.
He wants to transfer to Marion County
where McCall has fewer friends.

WARREN
Better than going to Miami. Three more
bombings since Labor Day! What's
taking the FBI so long?

THURGOOD

Your guess is as good as mine. We've
called everyone we can think of, twice,
and that includes the President and former
first lady! Unfortunately, we're standing
in a line that gets longer and longer every
day. They're moving Shepherd and Irvin
Tuesday night. You're welcome to attend
the hearing in Tavares Wednesday.

REESA

(stands and bolts to the living room)

Hi, Mr. Marshall! Nice to see you again,
sir! I couldn't help but hear... Can I
come too?

THURGOOD

That's up to your folks, Reesa.

REESA

Please, Daddy. Please.

WARREN

We'll discuss it later.

REESA

But Daddy...

WARREN
(to Thurgood)
Will there be trouble?

THURGOOD
You can count on it.

(lights dim)

(Lights come up on Dot, Elizabeth, Warren, and
Reesa sit at the kitchen table. All are very upset)

DOT
So what you're saying is he killed those
boys in cold blood!

WARREN
McCall swears they tried to run. He said
he had car trouble, and when he stopped,
they both tried to run.

DOT
I don't believe that for a minute.

WARREN
Neither do a lot of people. The thing is,
Lee Irvin was shot, but he survived. Once
he got to the hospital, he told the doctors

how McCall pulled off the road where no
one could see and turned and shot them
both. Dragged them out of the car
thinking they were dead. Samuel
Shepherd was dead.

ELIZABETH
I don't know how much more of this I can
stand, Warren.

WARREN
Well, now folks are starting to wonder
which one's telling the truth. Anybody
who knows McCall has a pretty good
idea. Maybe the FBI will finally look
into Klan activities here in Florida.

(A knock at the door.)

WARREN
(rises and open the door)
        Harry!

HARRY
I see by your faces, you heard about the
shooting.
(joins them at the table)

DOT
That's all anyone's talking about.

HARRY
Mark my words, they'll call it justifiable homicide! McCall's done this sort of thing before!

WARREN
This thing stinks to high heaven.

HARRY
I want to start a letter-writing campaign ~ ask the governor to remove McCall from office. I've written the first letter. I'm hoping you'll write one too.
(hands Warren his letter to read)

WARREN
Of course I will.

REESA
Me too!

HARRY
Florida's on trial before the whole world! Only prompt action by our governor can save the good name of our fair state.

WARREN

This is a great idea, Harry, but I hope
you're watching your back.

HARRY

There have been threats, but I've got a
thirty-two caliber in my car, and if it
comes to that, I'll take a few of them with
me.

REESA

They wouldn't hurt you, Mr. Harry.
You're too nice.

HARRY

That's not how everyone feels, Reesa.

WARREN

No. It's not.

(The lights in the house go black, and foliage
appears at the front of the stage. Nighttime
lighting appears over the foliage area. The
sounds of a Florida night are heard in the
background. Slowly, and deliberately, three
hooded figures in the white sheets and hoods of
the KKK enter from Stage Left. One unrolls two

cables from a place offstage while another carries
a plunger used for explosives.)

JOHN IVEY
You sure we used enough dynamite?

DONNELLY
(he attaches the cables from offstage to the
plunger as he speaks)
Course I'm sure! There's enough TNT
under that house to send them niggers to
the moon.

MORRIS BELLVIEW
I don't care where he lands as long as we
get that uppity Harry T. Moore.

JOHN IVEY
You sure it's in the right place?

DONNELLY
Would you quit worrying! You sound
like my maiden aunt! One of our boys
has been watching the house for days. He
drew up a diagram ~ same way we did it
in the war. That TNT we left just now is
right below Mr. and Mrs. Harry T.
Moore's bed. When they settle down for

their long winter's nap tonight, they'll get
the Christmas present to end all Christmas
presents!

MORRIS BELLVIEW

Ka-Boom!

DONNELLY

Right! Ka-Boom!
(Headlights swing past the men, and a car can be
heard pulling into the nearby driveway.)
Shhh! Get down.
(They crouch down in the weeds.)

JOHN IVEY

That them?

MORRIS BELLVIEW

Can you see?

DONNELLY

It's them alright!

JOHN IVEY

Hey, that's a kid! You didn't tell me they
had kids!

DONNELLY

Collateral damage. We wanna put an end
to all this black voting nonsense, Moore
has to go. It's his own fault if his family
gets hurt in the process. He started this.
Not us.

MORRIS BELLVIEW

Hurry up! Let's finish this.

JOHN IVEY

I think I'll wait at the car.

DONNELLY

Get back here. We're in this together!
We all agreed this had to be done! Just
give 'em a few minutes to settle in.

JOHN IVEY

No one said nothin' 'bout no kid!

DONNELLY

Who cares! Just another pickininny to
grow up and destroy our way of life.

MORRIS BELLVIEW

Look! Lights are out. Musta been a busy
day.

DONNELLY

Then let's send 'em to a real nice rest,
shall we, boys? An eternal one!
(He raises the plunger and depresses it. A large
flash and an explosion come from offstage.
Smoke pours out from the Stage Left entrance.
They grab the plunger and run. Lights out. Light
comes up on Reesa in her room. She has been
crying. Marvin is there.)

REESA

How? How could this happen, Marvin.
And on Christmas! It's like a nightmare!
Mr. Harry never hurt anybody. He was
one of the smartest, kindest people I ever
knew. He was going to get justice for
you, Marvin. Now, there's no one!

MARVIN

Sometimes other people don't want
justice, Reesa. They want justice buried
and forgotten, and sometimes they want it
bad enough to kill.

REESA

We're alone now, Marvin. With Mr.
Harry gone and Mr. Marshall back in
New York, how will we ever get rid of
the Klan?

MARVIN

I don't know, Reesa Rooster. I surely
don't, but God has a plan ~ something so
big we can't begin to understand.

REESA

How can you say that when everyone
around me keeps dying?

MARVIN

I don't claim to know the workin's of
God Almighty, Reesa. All's Ah know's
He's not finished here yet.

REESA
(hesitates)

Marvin?

MARVIN

What's on yo' mind, Reesa Roo?

REESA

Marvin, Mz. Lillian at the beauty shop…
She has a water fountain outside.

MARVIN

Ah seen it.

REESA

So you've seen the sign?

MARVIN

One dat reads "Whites Only"? Yeah, Ah
seen it.

REESA

Marvin, I'm ashamed. So ashamed!

MARVIN

Now, honey, why you ashamed? You
didn't put up dat sign!

REESA

That sign's been hanging there my whole
life, and my whole life, I never even saw
it until this happened to you!

MARVIN

Not surprisin'. Dat sign weren't meant
for you, so you didn't see it.

REESA

And Mz. Lillian. The way she goes on
and on about coloreds ~ like they ~ like
you're not people. She's done it every
time I've seen her all these years, and I
never even noticed it until now.

MARVIN

You're just a child, Rooster.

REESA

No, I'm not! Not anymore, and even if I
was, it's no excuse. There can never be
an excuse, Marvin! I feel just awful.

MARVIN

That's the way with the Klan, Reesa.
They sneaks up on ya a little at a time,
and before ya know it, you're helpin' 'em
along by ignorin' what they do. You still
ignorin' the Klan, Reesa?

REESA

God, no, Marvin. Never! Never again!

MARVIN
Then, I'd say dat's all we has to say on
dat subject.

REESA
I'm never using that fountain again,
Marvin! Never!

MARVIN
Dat, Reesa Roo, is a fine place to start!

Scene 3

(Sunrise in the kitchen. The tree is back to flowering which means spring has come. Reesa, Luther, and Warren sit eating breakfast. Elizabeth comes to the back door from outside. JAMESON follows her. He wears a dark suit and tie, and he has short hair. He carries a file folder.)

ELIZABETH
(Opens backdoor and comes in)
Warren, company.

WARREN
Everything alright?

ELIZABETH
(gestures to Jameson who has followed her into the kitchen)
This is Mr. James Jameson of the Federal Bureau of Investigation.

WARREN
(rises and shakes hands)
Warren McMahon. This is my daughter, Marie, and our friend Luther Cully.

JAMESON

Special Agent, Jim Jameson, in the flesh
as requested.

ELIZABETH

Excuse me. I left Robert in the
showroom. Told him I'd be right back.

JAMESON

Thank you, ma'am.

ELIZABETH

Reesa?

REESA

I'll be right there, Mama. I was just
finishing.

WARREN

Mr. Jameson, my assistant here…
(nods to Reesa)
Doesn't like me to talk to law
enforcement without seeing identification.

JAMESON

(smiles at the request)
Miss McMahon, my badge.

(reaches in his back pocket and pulls out his wallet)
>>And here's my card.
(hands card to Reesa)

WARREN
>>Where's he from, Reesa?

REESA
>>Well, his address says Orlando, but he sounds like Ohio to me.

JAMESON
>>Cleveland.

WARREN
>>We see a lot of tourists here. Reesa has made kind of a game of picking out the accent. Can we talk to him then?

REESA
>>Ohio should be safe.

JAMESON
>>Well, thank you, ma'am. Okay to sit here? I wanted to speak to Mr. Cully too, so this works out perfectly.
(looks at Reesa)

Your deputy staying?

WARREN
Reesa, don't you have some mending in
the living room?

REESA
(reluctantly)
Yes, sir.
(Reesa goes to living room. Grabs her mending
and tiptoes over to the wall where she listens in.
Marvin joins her. She is happy to see him, but
shushes him so they can listen.)

JAMESON
Mr. McMahon, Mr. Cully, I'm here to tell
you you have friends in high places.

WARREN
Really? Who would that be?

JAMESON
Let's start with my boss, Mr. Hoover.
And while we're at it we'll add Mr.
Thurgood Marshall of New York City.

WARREN
Okay...

JAMESON

And Mr. Cully, you're the father of
Marvin Cully, shot and killed last March?

LUTHER
(nervous)

Yes, sir.

JAMESON

Don't worry, Mr. Cully. You're not in
any trouble. Truth be told, I'm the one in
trouble.

WARREN

What do you mean?

JAMESON

Well, as you know, two people were
assassinated by dynamite over six weeks
ago. So far, my agents have very little
evidence and almost no suspects. Mr.
Hoover is not happy, especially since his
boss, Mr. Truman and a lot of other
influential people are breathing down his
neck for answers.

WARREN

Is that so?

JAMESON

Believe me. It's very much so.

WARREN

What's this have to do with us?

JAMESON

We're operating in a bit of a vacuum here. Although your state's law enforcement departments have promised their full cooperation, they've done next to nothing to help us get to the bottom of this. In spite of that fact, we have extremely compelling reasons to believe the Apopka Klan has direct knowledge of the murders of Mr. and Mrs. Moore. The problem is, we have no inside sources. According to Mr. Marshall, you have a good handle on what's going on around here, Mr. McMahon. I don't suppose you'd consider joining the Klan for us?

WARREN

Me? A Klanner? Mr. Jameson, I'm a Yankee for starters, and a man who speaks his mind loud and long. Even if they'd have me, which I doubt, I couldn't do it. It'd take me ~ what do you think,

Luther ~ maybe three, four minutes tops
to blow my cover?

JAMESON

I've thought you might say that. Mr.
Marshall also says between you and Mr.
Cully you have a circle of friends who,
let's see how'd he say that, put the FBI
and the CIA to shame.

WARREN

That's mostly Luther's choir.

LUTHER

The choir ladies work in the homes of the
Klanners. They tells us what the Klan is
up to or what they's braggin' about just
finishin'.

JAMESON

What I'd like to ask you is this, I have a
list of names we believe to be members of
the Apopka Klan, cross-referenced from
several sources. I'd like you to look over
this list and have your circle of friends
look it over too. Cross off anyone who's
not a known Klan member and add
anyone whose name should appear on the

list. Is that something you can do to help us catch whoever killed Marvin Cully and the Moores?

                    WARREN

If we agree to look at your list, Mr. Jameson, what happens to it when we're done with it?

                    JAMESON

I've thought about that. I've placed two pieces of paper in this envelope.
(holds up large manial envelope)
          The first sheet is the list. The second is a short summary of events that occurred last summer ~ a speed chase between a black Chrysler and three pickups. Did you see it?

                    WARREN

Didn't everybody?

                    JAMESON

The second sheet merely describes the incident. If you could add any comments that might flesh out the details, it'd be a big help to my investigation. As you can see, the envelope's stamped and addressed to Mr. James Smith at my post office box in Orlando. All you have to do is look things over, make your comments, seal it, and mail it back as soon as you can.

                    WARREN
We'll take a look.

                    LUTHER
We hasta do more than look, MistaWarren. That's my son they kilt.

                    WARREN
You're right, Luther. I didn't want to commit you without us discussing it first. It could be dangerous.

                    LUTHER
I knows the color of mah skin, MistaWarren. Can't be no mo' dangerous helpin' the FBI than it is just livin' here now.

                    JAMESON
                  (hesitates)
So you're in?

WARREN

Yes.
(sensing Jameson's hesitation)
        Is there something else?

JAMESON

We've heard the Klan has their
headquarters in an old fishing camp near
here. Do you know it?

LUTHER

Must be the place on Boy Scout Road.
Couldn't be no other.

JAMESON

That's the place. We've had one source
tell us there's a hidden compartment
inside the fishing camp building which
holds documents ~ documents that could
bring down the entire Klan.

WARREN

So why don't you get them?

JAMESON

No judge in this county will give us a
warrant. What we're talking about here

... To be honest, it'd be breaking and
entering.
(silence as Luther and Warren look at each other)

WARREN
I'll do it.

JAMESON
We sort of see this as a two man job. One
to go in and find the compartment and
one to stand watch.

LUTHER
I'll go too.

REESA
(runs in)
Oh, Daddy! No! They'll kill you both!

WARREN
(ignores Reesa)
But, Luther, it's the Klan's headquarters.
If we're caught...

LUTHER
I know, MistaWarren. We'll just be sure
we don't get caught.

                    JAMESON
                    (looks at Warren)
It's your call.

                    WARREN
How much time do we have?

                    JAMESON
Why?

                    WARREN
We can go the next moonless night which
is eight days from now.

                    REESA
(grabs Warren's arm, pleading)
But…

                    JAMESON
You've got that, but not much more. The
US Attorney General has agreed to
convene a grand jury in Miami the first
week of April. We'll be presenting
everything we have on the Apopka Klan
and its involvement in the deaths of the
Moores and the other bombings in Miami.

WARREN

Finally! Do I call when I have it?

JAMESON

No. No calls. Use the envelope. Uh, I'm authorized to pay you two hundred and fifty dollars for your trouble.

WARREN

I don't want your money, Mr. Jameson.

LUTHER

Me neither. Ain't takin' nothin' for getting' justice for mah boy!

REESA

But, Luther! Marvin wouldn't want this! He wouldn't want you risking your lives for him!

LUTHER

Hasta be done, Roo. Not jus' for Marvin. For all of us. You see how it is. I know you do.

REESA
(reluctantly)

Yes. I see.

WARREN
(to Jameson)
You can do us a favor though.

JAMESON
What's that?

WARREN
Strike my name and Luther's from your
files. I don't want anyone getting word
we had anything to do with this. Who
knows what they'd do if they found out.

JAMESON
(nods)
Warren… if you get caught, I never heard
of you.

WARREN
I understand. Will we see you again?

JAMESON
No. Not if everything goes right. You're
doing a tremendous service, Warren.
Luhter.

WARREN
Lets' hope so.

REESA
(echoes)
Let's hope so.

Scene 4

Scene starts in the kitchen of the McMahon house. It is nighttime, eight nights later. A moveable set of trees and brush which fold up and down is on the apron area at the front of the stage. For now, the trees are down, and the set looks as it has throughout the play. This scene cuts back and forth between the indoor and outdoor sets. When action takes place in the outdoor set, lights dim in the kitchen and action freezes. When action takes place in the indoor set, lights are black on the outdoor set, trees and shrubs fold back down, and the outdoor actors step offstage.

Warren stand at the back door in dark clothes and acting as if nothing special is about to happen. Elizabeth and Reesa play cards at the table. Elizabeth is especially stiff and tense.

WARREN
Luther! Come on in!
(spots Armetta behind Luther)
You too, Armetta?

ARMETTA

Luther and I thought y'all could use a
little company while the men are out
gallivantin'. Were we wrong?

ELIZABETH

Not at all. Thank you. I appreciate you
thinking of us.

ARMETTA

Thinkin' of myself too. Waitin's hard
work 'less you have comp'ny to distract
you.

LUTHER

Where's Mz. Dot?

WARREN

She took off to the movies. She figured
it'd be less stressful for Lizbeth if she's
out of the house tonight.

LUTHER

Good thinkin'. Ah, believe we could do
with a word of prayer befo' we go.

WARREN

I think so too, Luther.

(They all join hands.)

LUTHER
All right then… Lawd, You know our
hearts, and You know we have no hope of
accomplishin' our task tonight without
Your help. We feel, Lawd, like Joshua
when You took him to the great walls of
Jericho and told him to let Your trumpets
blow! Blow those trumpet, You said, and
the walls of Jericho will come a tumblin'
down. Old Joshua believed You, Lawd,
and so do we. We ask you tonight to lay
that trumpet in our hands. We all know
our part, Lawd, and we gonna do the best
we can, but guide our steps, and protect
our path. Show us the secret hidin' place,
and Lawd, lay that trumpet in our hands!
We thank you for your help and for the
hope that fills our hearts tonight. We
bless you for the privilege of doin' this in
your name, and we praise You, Lawd,
tonight and forever. Amen.

WARREN, ARMETTA, & ELIZABETH
Amen.

REESA

Amen.

WARREN

(turns to Elizabeth)

We'll stick to the plan. Luther's spies tell
us the Apopka Klan is at some big rally in
Orlando tonight, so the place should be
empty. Why, it won't even get
interesting, Lizbeth.

ELIZABETH

They could come back any time and head
straight out to that fishing camp, Warren,
and you know it!

WARREN

We figured it all out. Even if they come
back… The trip to and from Orlando will
take a while. As long as we're out by ten
thirty, there's no risk at all.

ELIZABETH

Which gets you home when?

WARREN

Eleven o'clock. Not one minute later. I
promise. Lizbeth, please don't worry.
We have to do this.

ELIZABETH

You haven't been in a lake since you
caught the polio from swimming in a
Florida lake the year Reesa was born. I
can't believe you're going to wade
through one in the dark tonight. You
know how dangerous it is!

WARREN
(laughs a bit)
I know, but it's the only way. We'll
sneak in the back way through the dump.
We can leave the truck there, and no one
will ever see it. Eleven o'clock, Lizbeth.
(They hug)
Trust me.

ELIZABETH

Eleven o'clock then.
(The clock on the kitchen wall reads nine
o'clock. Elizabeth checks it.)

ARMETTA
Reesa, I brought the dry goods for makin'
snicker doodles. Thought you could help
me by writin' down the measures. Can
you do dat, Roo?

(Luther and Warren exit with a wave. Elizabeth
returns sternly to her cards on the table. This
time she plays solitaire.)

REESA
I'll get some paper.
(goes to living room and gets paper and a pencil.)

ARMETTA
Might as well do something useful while
we'se sittin' here worryin'.

ELIZABETH
Might as well.

ARMETTA
Now, Reesa Roo, let's start with the flour.
Do you have some eggs?

REESA
Yes'm.

(opens the refrigerator door as lights dim and
action freezes. Trees and bushes come up, and
Luther and Warren appear at the edge of the
stage. They carry small flashlights which they
sweep around in the dark. They walk together.)

LUTHER
Sho' stinks out here, MistaWarren.

WARREN
Sure does, Luther. We'll get used to it.
Come on, the lake's this way.

LUTHER
That saw grass is mighty sharp. Cuttin'
my arms somethin' fierce. You don't
suppose they's gonna be gators in this
lake, do ya, MistaWarren?

WARREN
Wouldn't surprise me, Luther.
(Luther steps into the lead and shines his light
high while Warren keeps his light on the path in
front of Luther.)

LUTHER
You think dem gators can smell this
blood, MistaWarren?

WARREN

No. They're probably all asl... Freeze
right there, Luther. Don't move!
(Luther freezes stock still ~ his foot poised to
step.)

LUTHER

What? What is it?

WARREN

Just stand real still, Luther. Point your
flashlight right where you were going
step.

LUTHER

God, Awmighty! What *is* that thing?

WARREN

That's a water moccasin. Looks like he
doesn't care for the light in his eyes.
Wait. Hold still. Looks like you sacred
him off, Luther!

LUTHER

No more than he sacred me! Don't
wanna mess with his kind tonight. And
here I was worryin' 'bout gators.

WARREN

Still plenty to worry about when we get to
the lake. I've got nine twenty-five,
Luther. Let's keep track of the time.
Don't want any unpleasant surprises.

LUTHER

No, sirree. No, we don't.

(Outdoor set goes black as Warren and Luther
reach the other side of the stage. The trees and
shrubs fold down and lights come up in the
kitchen.

ARMETTA

(she and Reesa are laughing and having a great
time. Elizabeth sits stone-faced with her cards at
the table. The clock says 9:47)

So then, Marvin says to me, Mamma, I
likes the batter better anyhow. Well, I
warned him eatin' them cookies befo'
they cooked ain't good for his belly, but
you know Marvin. I turned mah back for
five minutes, and that boy plum ate all the
cookie dough and run off outside. Wasn't
an hour later he come back 'pologizin'
and wailin' 'bout the belly ache he had.

REESA

Sounds just like Marvin.

ARMETTA

Yep. That boy always did have to learn
things the hard way.

REESA

I'll never forget the story he told me
about Miss Angel Blossom and Mister
Bee.

ARMETTA

Marvin loved that story. Tol' it good too.
He'd of made a fine preacher or a lawyer
like Mistuh Marshall.

REESA

Marvin, a lawyer. Wouldn't that have
been something?

ARMETTA

Course, I never would have thought it 'til
I met Mistuh Moore and Mistuh Marshall.
Still a hor'ble shame what happened to
the Moores. They was fine people. Met
his wife at a voter registration class at

their house in Brevard. She was a lovely
woman.
(silence)
Okay, so this is the bakin' powder, Roo.
(She measures the baking powder and dumps it
into an empty bowl.)
How much?

REESA
(measures the powder in the bowl into a large
bowl with cookie dough in it using a tablespoon.)
Looks like three tablespoons, Armetta.

ARMETTA
Write dat down, Roo. One thing I've
learnt this year. Write down the things
dat's important if you wants to keep 'em.

(lights dim in the kitchen and the women freeze
as the trees and shrubs fold up on the apron of the
stage. Luther and Warren are back at the same
side of the stage where they started last time and
continuing to move forward. This time, there is a
tiny shack standing at the other end of the stage.
It needs only have a door that can be opened.
The audience does not see inside.)

LUTHER

We're getting' close now. Ah don't see
no lights, MistaWarren.

WARREN

Me either. That's a good sign.

LUTHER

Don't look like much, do it?

WARREN

I'll try the door. You keep an eye out for
anything. You see lights on that service
road, Luther. Whistle.

LUTHER

Like this?
          (whistles)

WARREN

Perfect. Wish me luck.
(He enters the shack as Luther watches nervously
from outside. Warren lets out a long, low
whistle.)

LUTHER

What is it, MistaWarren? Ah thought
Ah's the one s'posed to whistle.

WARREN

Look at this, Luther. Can you believe
this? I never...

LUTHER

Me either. Who'd've ever thought...
Lawd, Lawd, Ah hope you find dem
papers quick-like. I can just imagine the
devil hisself sittin' in that fancy throne
chair. This place gives me the willies.

WARREN

Okay. Keep a sharp eye out for anything.

LUTHER

Ah plan to. Ah's not int'rested in meetin'
up with any of dat fat ol' snake's larger
relations tonight.
(he shines his beam around the room and over the
audience. Then he flips off the flashlight and sits
down to wait. It isn't long before tapping is hear
from inside the shack.)
Mista Warren, dat you?

WARREN
(from inside the shack)
I'm looking for a secret compartment, a
false wall ~ somewhere they'd hide their
records.

LUTHER
(whispers loudly)
Anthing yet?

WARREN
(still tapping)
Nothing! Jameson isn't going to be too
happy if we come out of this empty-
handed.
(Hard tap and movement of wood is heard)
Wait! Luther! Luther! I found a hole. A
tackle box. They're so arrogant, there's
no lock! Books ~ papers!
(emerges from the shack as Luther switches on
his flashlight)
Look at this, Luther!
(he holds up a metal tackle box which he has
opened. A Bible lays on top of some papers and
a bank pouch.)

LUTHER

(Takes the Bible and reads)

   Presented to Mr. Reed Garnet on the
   occasion of his confirmation in the
   Apopka Presbyterian Church. Lawd, oh
   Lawd!

WARREN

Age twelve, by his loving mother. Oh,
Lord. Wouldn't Hannah Garnet just die if
she knew where this Bible ended up?

LUTHER

Maybe... And maybe not.

WARREN

We'll leave the pouch. I don't want their
money. Don't want to be accused of
burglary, but these papers look
interesting... and the Bible.

LUTHER

What's dat one, Mista Warren?

WARREN

God, Luther, it's their membership list.
And this is a treasury record... attendance
log. It's all here! Documented proof of

every member of the Apopka Klan! This
is it, Luther! Jameson'll have everything
he needs to take them down!

(A car door slams in the distance, and Warren
and Luther douse the lights and crouch down.
They are terrified. Lights come back up on the
kitchen as the shrubbery folds down and Luther
and Warren exit quickly in the same direction
they entered from. Armetta and Reesa join
Elizabeth at the table now. A heaping plate of
cookies sits in the middle of the table.)

REESA
Have you always lived in Plymouth,
Armetta?

ARMETTA
Oh, no, chil'. I was born and raised in
Ocoee.

REESA
Ocoee! But there aren't any Negroes in
Ocoee!

ARMETTA
Not now, but there used to be a whole
community, like The Quarters here in
Plymouth, only bigger.

REESA

What happened to it?

ARMETTA

Election Day 1920 happened, Rooster.
And a man named Mose Norman, my
neighbor, drove downtown to vote. The
local Klan was mostly Dixiecrat, and they
were worried because most Negroes were
votin' Republican. The Klan showed up
at the polls and started pushin' and
shovin' our people away. Well, Mose
Norman got hit, and that made him mad.
Mose drove ova' to O'landah to complain
to a lawyer named Cheney.

REESA

What happened then?

ARMETTA

Well, Mr. Cheney tol' Mose to drive back
to Ocoee and write down the names of
anyone interferin' with the vote and
anyone else who got turned away. Long
story short, it turned into a mob scene,
and that night, the Klan showed up and
set fire to our houses.

REESA

Oh, Armetta, no.

ELIZABETH

I remember hearing about it. The locals
called it the Ocoee Riot.

ARMETTA

They called it a lot of things. Most of it
untrue. Anyhow, there was a big gun
battle at the home of July Perry. Ol' July
lived in the middle of a grove, and he was
the most influential Negro in town. He
hadn't done a thing, but the Klan came
after him sayin' he was hidin' ol' Mose
up in his house. Course, by then, Mose
was long gone.

REESA

Smart man.

ARMETTA

July asked to see they search warrant, and
the Klan just opened fire. He tried to
fight back, but the mob came and got him.
Strung up ol' July Perry in a oak tree
outside his house.

ELIZABETH

Armetta!

ARMETTA

The rest of us jus' scattered, scared outta our wits by burnin' crosses and flamin' houses. For a couple hours, me, Mamma and Daddy, and my brothers and sisters hid out in a grove listenin' to the sound of gunfire and people yellin' and cryin'. When Daddy decided it was safe to move, we started walkin' in the pitch-dark. We made it to Plymouth jus' after dawn, and mah cousins took us in.

REESA

How old were you?

ARMETTA

A year younger than you are now, Reesa.

ELIZABETH

But your things? Your property?

ARMETTA

No one ever went back. At first we were too scared. Then, we just didn't care.

(The sound of the DeSoto coming up the drive
breaks the spell.)

REESA
Must be Dot! That means Daddy and
Luther'll be home soon.

(Elizabeth checks the clock which says 10:37.
Dot comes in through the back door.)

DOT
That Cary Grant is such a doll! I swear,
his smile could melt butter! Are they
back yet?

ELIZABETH
(harsh)
No. No, they're not back yet.

REESA
Armetta and I made cookies, Dot.

DOT
Hi Armetta. Nice to see you again.

ARMETTA
You too, Mz. Dot!

DOT

They should be right behind me. Warren
was certain they'd be home by eleven.

ELIZABETH

So he said.

(The ticking of the clock can be heard, and the
clock speeds forward to 11:15. Elizabeth paces
between the living room and kitchen with worry
as the others sit at the table watching the clock in
the kitchen.)

REESA

Something's wrong! I just know it!

DOT

Calm down. Your daddy's smarter than
ten of those men put together. He'll be
here.

REESA

But, what if you're wrong? Oh, Dot...

ARMETTA

Mz. Dot's right, Reesa. Dem boys
prob'ly jus' took longer to fin' dem
papers than your daddy 'spected.

ELIZABETH

It's a ten minute drive. Where could they
possibly be?

(Ticking of clock is louder and again the clock
moves to 11:30.)

DOT

They really should be here by now.
Maybe I should take the car, and…

REESA

No, Dot! No! Don't go out there! I
couldn't bear to lose you too!

ELIZABETH

Nobody's lost! They're just running
behind. Isn't that right, Armetta?

ARMETTA

Absolutely! Why, we can't know what's
happenin' out there..

REESA

But what if…

(The sound of the truck pulling up outside brings
everyone to their feet and crowding around the

back door. Reesa flies out the door and greets
Luther and Warren.)

REESA

God, Daddy! We thought the Klan got
you for sure!

(Warren and Luther walk to the door and into the
kitchen. They are wet from about the chest
down. Warren stops to give Elizabeth a
reassuring hug.)

DOT

We thought no such thing, Warren, but I
am glad to see you.
(to the room)
See, they're fine.

WARREN

Glad to be home. Tire! Goddamn tire
went flat! Must've picked up a nail on
the way in. Flatter than a pancake when
we got back.

LUTHER

Right as rain now!

WARREN

And just about as wet. Sorry for scaring you all. Everything went fine until that tire. Never changed a tire so fast in my life.

LUTHER

We heard a car too, but was just some ol' man come down to fish.

WARREN

Scared us good!

LUTHER

Everyone of dem Klanners must've been at that big rally downtown.

WARREN

The lake wasn't but three and half feet deep. We waded right across. But Luther nearly stepped on a water moccasin on the way in.

ARMETTA

Oh, Luther! Thank God you're all right!

ELIZABETH

What about the shack?

WARREN

We were expecting a padlock or
something, but I tried the handle, and the
door opened easy as you please. We
walked right in!

LUTHER

Tell 'em 'bout *dat*!

WARREN

Damnedest thing I've ever seen. On the
outside, the building's just a plain pine
clapboard shack, badly in need of
painting. Inside, it looked like a
cathedral. Polished tongue-in-groove
cypress paneled all the way around like in
a church or a courtroom.

LUTHER

You wouldn't believe it!

WARREN

Black, red, and gold everywhere. Like a
House of Horrors with a big square
painted on the floor. An altar of some
kind stood in the middle of the square.

LUTHER
Gave me the shivers!

WARREN
The whole place made my skin crawl.
Luther went back out to keep watch, and I
started hammering on panels ~ looking
for a hollow place. Took about ten
minutes to find a hidden door in the
woodwork. Inside we found this!
(He lays the papers and books, including the
Bible on the table for all to see.)

REESA
What are they, Daddy?

WARREN
(feigns disappointment)
Not much.
(delighted)
Just Membership and Attendance Records
and the Tresurer's log for the entire
Apopka Klan!
(places books on the table)

DOT

If that doesn't beat all! That should help
Mr. Jameson put an end to their
shenanigans!
(she picks up the books Warren places on the
table)

REESA

Then what happened?

WARREN

When we heard that fisherman we
thought we were done for. We high-
tailed it out of there and found the truck.
When we spotted the flat, it seemed like
everything had turned against us. Luther
checked on the fisherman, and I changed
the tire. And here we are!

REESA

Were you scared, Daddy?

WARREN

Terrified.

REESA

You too, Luther?

LUTHER

More than Ah've ever been in mah whole
life, Roo.

ARMETTA

(looking at the book Dot holds in her hand)
Those last two sheets of paper are loose in
dat book. What are they?

DOT

(unfolds the pages)
This first one's an invitation to the rally
tonight. It calls on good Democrats and
real southerners to support Eisenhower
for President and tells them where to meet
in Orlando.

WARREN

Jim Jameson was right. This stuff is
going to help the grand jury make a lot of
changes around here.

DOT

(unfolds the other paper)
This one looks like a floor plan.

ARMETTA

May I?

(looks at the paper. Then
awareness dawns)

Oh, sweet Jesus!

ELIZABETH

What, Armetta? What is it?

ARMETTA

When I was working with Mr. Moore, Ah
went out to his house a few times for
classes on teaching coloreds how to vote.
This is dey house.

DOT

What are you saying?

ARMETTA

This is the floor plan for Mr. and Mrs.
Moore's house fo' sho'. This is what
they used to kill the head of the N double
A C P!

Scene 5

(Night time in the McMahon house. Dot sits
reading a book in the living room, and Reesa,
Elizabeth, and Warren sit playing cards in the
kitchen.)

                    WARREN
                    (throws down his cards)
        Gin!

                    REESA
        Again! Daddy, you're the luckiest man in
        the whole world!

(Suddenly the lights go out in the house, and
lights like torches are seen outside. Dot rushes
into the kitchen.)

                    DOT
        Warren, what is it?

                    WARREN
        I don't know. Somebody's out there.

                    ELIZABETH
        How'd they cut the lights?

(A rock breaks the window and lands in the
kitchen. Then another. Reesa picks up one of
the rocks and looks at it in disbelief.)

                    WARREN
        Get down. Everybody, get down now.
        Reesa, take your mother and grandma to
        the back of the house.

                    REESA
        But, Daddy!

                    DOT
        We can get there ourselves.
(Elizabeth and Dot head down the hall to a back
bedroom)

                    WARREN
        Reesa, give me that rock!

                    REESA
        You can't go out there, Daddy! They
        know! They know!

                    WARREN
        They're just a bunch of cowards in white
        sheets. They're not used to anyone
        standing up to them. Give me that rock.

(Reesa passes the rock to her father. The
torchlight has gone around to the side of the
house, and Warren is able to open the kitchen
door without being seen. He takes the rock and
throws it hard. A yelp of pain is heard offstage.)
        Now, the other one!
(Reesa picks up the second rock, Warren throws
again, and again a yowl of pain is heard offstage.
To Reesa)
            There's only two of them. It's not the
            whole Klan!
(yells outside)
            Don't make me get my gun! Looks like
            that leg'll be pretty sore this week! I'd
            hate to add to it with a load of buckshot,
            but I will if you push me.

                JOHN IVEY(offstage)
            Let's get outta here! Emmett'll deal with
            him!

                (Yells loudly to Warren)
            This ain't over! We know it was you!
            This ain' over!

(Reesa runs to her father and hugs him close.
Elizabeth and Dot returns to the darkened kitchen
where Elizabeth sees the broken glass, shakes her
head, and starts cleaning up.)

DOT

They know, Warren.

WARREN

They only think they know. There's no proof.

DOT

But why you?

WARREN

Makes sense. Marvin worked for me. His father's my friend and foreman. We're the only Yankee family in the county. Who else?

ELIZABETH

Does it matter?

WARREN

I think it does.

REESA

What are you going to do, Daddy?

WARREN

What I should have done a long time ago,
Reesa. I'm going to meet with Emmett
Casselton and lay out the options. It's
time we get some things squared away
and evening visits to my family in my
home is at the top of the list!

ELIZABETH

They're going to kill you too, Warren.

WARREN

I wouldn't be so sure. You see, I have an
ace in the hole.

(Lights dim as the set for the Lakeview Inn is
brought back onstage. EMMETT CASSELTON
stands by one of the booths. Reesa follws
Warren into the restaurant and hides behind a
booth to watch. No one else is in the restaurant.
Warren enters. Reesa follows behind him unseen
by Emmett. Warren motions to her to stay
behind the wall and keep down before he faces
Emmett.)

WARREN

Emmett, good of you to meet me.

(Emmett stands quietly watching Warren)

Had a visit from your friends the other night. Unfortunately I had to cut their stay short.

EMMETT

You got somethin' to say, McMahon, get to it. Otherwise, I've got business.

WARREN

The way I see it, your men started this thing. They took my foreman's son and murdered him in cold-blood. You'd have done the same thing I did to protect your own.

EMMETT

Maybe.

WARREN

At that point, I would've called us even, but clearly you didn't agree. You sent those boys to my house, which unfortunately, Emmett, makes it my turn. I know a few things, Emmett.

(Emmet squints menacingly.)

EMMETT

Such as?

WARREN

For instance, I know the FBI took all your
dynamite, but what you may not know is
they didn't take mine. You see, I'm not
in the habit of terrorizing my neighbors,
so they left me *plenty* ~ enough to blow
one or two buildings sky high! There's
your fishing camp, of course. And there's
the building you own in downtown
Apopka. And I know your warehouse
over on Votaw Road. What I thought,
Emmett, since you made it my turn, you
could help me decide...

EMMETT

You threatenin' me, McMahon?

WARREN

Not at all. But you're the exalted Cyclops
or whatever they call you ~ the big
decision maker, right? Who better to help
decide where we go from here?

EMMETT

Where would you like us to go?

WARREN

That depends on you…

EMMETT

You askin' me to pick?

WARREN

I'm asking your opinion ~ looking for
advice. You could say here or there, or
you could suggest something else
entirely.

EMMETT

What's that supposed to mean?

WARREN

You could surprise me by declaring this
thing over, right here, right now. We
could make an agreement it's ended. Of
course, I'd need your word on it as a
gentleman. You give me yours. I'll give
you mine. Then we'd both be done with
this.

EMMETT

What guarantee do I have you'll keep
yours?

WARREN

I figured you might have a problem with
the word of a Yankee. I could arrange to
deliver your guarantee in say, fifteen
minutes. You wait right here, and I'll do
that.

EMMETT

What kind of guarantee?

WARREN

You'll have to trust me on that, Emmett.
Do we have a deal or not?
(Emmett reaches out his hand and shakes with
Warren without saying a word.)
Stay right here. Fifteen minutes.
(Warren exits and Reesa sneaks out and runs
after her father. Lights dim as restaurant set is
removed and comes up on Reesa and Warren
outside their house. The have a small red wagon
next to them with a tarp over the top. A single
stick of dynamite sticks out from under the tarp.)

WARREN

That's all of it!

REESA
(unsure of Warren's methods)
Are you sure, Daddy? All of it?

WARREN
If we don't use it all, my word won't be
worth much. Will it, Roo?

REESA
I just thought maybe we should keep a
little. Just in case…

WARREN
There is no 'just in case', Reesa. This is
all or nothing. How much time?

REESA
Four minutes.

WARREN
Okay. Let's head for the hills.

REESA
Is that far enough, Daddy?

WARREN
We'll be fine, Reesa. Just stay behind
that rock when we're ready.

(They walk away dragging the full wagon behind them, and there is silence for a beat. Suddenly, there is the sound of a horrific explosion. Dot and Elizabeth race to the windows at the back of the house. Reesa and Warren return to the house through the kitchen door. Elizabeth throws open the back door when she sees Reesa and Warren approaching.)

ELIZABETH
Warren McMahon, what on earth was that explosion?

WARREN
Me keeping my word.
(to Reesa)
How'd we do on time?

REESA
Fifteen minutes exactly!

ELIZABETH
Warren, is there anything left of our grove?

WARREN

Actually, we stacked all the dynamite in
that dry sinkhole, and you won't believe
this, but the explosion knocked something
loose.

ELIZABETH

Oh, I'd believe it!

WARREN

There's a lake out back again, and if I
know Emmett Casselton, we have an
agreement with the Klan too.

ELIZABETH

Really, Warren?

WARREN

What's your take on the matter, Reesa?

REESA

If I had to guess, I'd say we've heard the
last of the Apopka Klan!

(Lights out)

Scene 6

(Reesa and Marvin stand in her bedroom. She
reaches up and gives him a big hug. Elizabeth
and Warren sit in the kitchen playing a card game
and drinking coffee.)

                REESA
    Isn't it wonderful, Marvin? The grand
    jury indicted nine members of the Apopka
    Klan! And they got five more from
    Orlando, Ocoee, and Miami! They
    prosecutor's been showing the floor plan
    of the Moore's house and talking about
    how it was used to set the bomb that
    killed them. Daddy's a hero, but Mr.
    Jameson kept his word. There's been no
    mention of Daddy or Luther since the trial
    started!

                MARVIN
    That's wonderful news, Roo. Any word
    on a murder trial for J.D. Bowman?

                REESA
    No. The grand jury doesn't have
    jurisdiction for murder, and no one in the
    state will arrest him for what he did.
    There's no evidence. Daddy says the

coroner probably got rid of the bullet
from J.D. Bowman's gun.

MARVIN
Is it over then, Roo? Is it really over?

REESA
I guess so. Mr. Reed Garnet's been
giving testimony before the grand jury,
and the Apopka Klan's running scared.
Daddy says the grand jury said the KKK
was founded on the worst instincts of
mankind.

MARVIN
They got that right.

REESA
He said they were intolerant and bigoted
and at times sadistic and brutal.

MARVIN
They got that right too.

REESA

None of those men is going to jail for
murder, Marvin. No one's being held
accountable for what they did to you. Or
to the Moores!

MARVIN

Reesa, do you think it'll ever be biz'ness
as usual for them Klanners ever again?

REESA

No, Marvin. They don't dare. Daddy put
the fear of God into Emmett Casselton!
Your mamma told my mamma the wives
and mothers of those Klanners have had it
up to here with their tom-foolery! The
womenfolk have put an end to the
Apopka Klan!

MARVIN

Then, maybe I don't need no trial.

REESA

But, Marvin! It's not right!

MARVIN

Course it's not right, but I tol' you before, those men'll face the Lawd God Awmighty Hisself one day, and we both know his justice is swift and merciless. Until then, they's never gonna be able to do to anyone what they done to me.

REESA

I guess that's right. From what Daddy said, the eyes of the entire world are on Florida now.

MARVIN

So let it go.

REESA

What do you mean?

MARVIN

I mean, let it go. Let me go, Reesa. Ah got nothin' else to do here, and Ah'm plum tuckered out. I don't need a murder trial to get justice. Gawd'll handle that, and I'll be there to see it.

REESA

But I can't let you go, Marvin. You're
my best friend!

MARVIN

And you're mine, but it's time I became
what I am ~ just a memory. Just the
happy memory of all those years we spent
together, Roo.

REESA

Will you be there ~ in heaven, I mean ~
when it's my time, Marvin?

MARVIN

I wouldn't miss it for the world. In the
meantime, you got big things to do with
your life, Reesa. You gonna be
somethin'!

REESA

I am?

MARVIN

Yo sho are! Just, don't forget, Reesa.
Don't forget your ol' friend Marvin, and
if you can, don't let no one else forget

either. They's a lesson here, Rooster.
Make sure it's not lost.

                    REESA
I'll try, Marvin. I'll try.
(hugs him and cries)
        Good bye, Marvin.

                    MARVIN
        Bye, Rooter-Tooter-Where's-Yo-Scooter!
        See you in the funny papers!
(Marvin slips into Reesa's closet, and she is
alone in her room. She watches Marvin exit, and
wipes at a tear. She takes a deep breath and exits
to the kitchen where Warren drops an arm around
her waist as she comes up next to him. He
studies her face a moment.)

                    WARREN
    What? What is it, Reesa?

                    REESA
I'm happy, Daddy.

                    WARREN
That's always good to hear. Any
particular reason?

REESA

Marvin.

WARREN

Marvin?

REESA

He's at peace, Daddy. His spirit's in
heaven, and he's finally at peace. Thank
you, Daddy. Thank you.

(Warren can only hug Reesa in response.)

(CURTAIN)

Made in United States
Orlando, FL
27 January 2023

29118748R00108